Very Nice Things People are Saying about James Finn Garner:

"James Finn Garner isn't a mere writer; he's a virtuoso, a necromancer, a master of the tour de force."
Jonathan Yardley, *Washington Post*

"Hillary and I have been enjoying your *Politically Correct Bedtime Stories,* and we look forward to your future work. . . . I've given several copies to others — it's hilarious!"
President Bill Clinton

"Garner has a smart, tart and often on-target sense of humor. And plenty of people are laughing."
Valerie Takahama, *Orange County Register*

"A master of modern satire."
Cleveland Plain Dealer

Other Books by James Finn Garner

Double Indignity:
A Rex Koko, Private Clown Mystery

The Wet Nose of Danger:
A Rex Koko, Private Clown Mystery

Tea Party Fairy Tales
A Kindle Single Exclusive!

Politically Correct Bedtime Stories
International Best-Seller!
60 Weeks on NY Times Best-Seller List,
including 8 weeks at #1!

Once Upon a More Enlightened Time
NY Times Best-Seller!

Politically Correct Holiday Stories
NY Times Best-Seller!

Apocalypse Wow!
A Memoir for the End of Time

Recut Madness:
Favorite Movies Retold for
Your Partisan Pleasure

For more information, visit JamesFinnGarner.com

HONK HONK,

My Darling

HONK HONK,
My Darling

A Rex Koko,
Private Clown Mystery

by James Finn Garner

Based on the characters created in the Waveland Radio Playhouse by James Finn Garner and Pat Byrnes

"Clown Alley Sally" words and music by Pat Byrnes

Cover design and layout by Airan Wright

Back cover illustration by Tony Akins

ISBN: 978-1468087086

Brought to you by Suddsy Soap,
The *Cleeeeean* Soap in the Handy Paste!

Dedicated to Pat Byrnes, Dan Shea
and Jordan Polansky, when the
rehearsals were more fun
than the performances,

And, til it's all out and over,
to Lies.

"To be up on the wire is to live.
Everything else is just waiting."

— *Karl Wallenda*

"Damn everything, but the circus!"

— *e. e. cummings*

CHAPTER 1

Dealing from the Bottom

When world-renowned flier Reynaldo Carlozo began whacking the soles of my feet, I was having a nice roll in the hay. If only I hadn't been there by my lonesome, something worthwhile might've come from this whole larry. As it was, this was just another rude awakening in a dingy locale.

"Koko! Koko!" he barked. "Come on, wake up! Get out of there!"

When he was up, working the trapeze, Carlozo was the epitome of control, strength and grace, a fearless deity in a spangly leotard, Icarus' younger, better-looking brother. The King of the Air, he was billed. Any other time than up, he was a mean, arrogant kinker with a brushfire temper and a talent for aggravation. If you're curious, the last time he flew in a show was five years ago.

"What th' hell's goin' on? Let a clown sleep, f'r chrissake." Waking up was going to be grueling whenever I did it today, but my hangover was quite capable of doing its job without anybody's help. You think your mouth is dry the morning after? See how it feels after sleeping all night in an elephant stall.

"Get up, get up! We need to talk!" he barked, hitting me on the feet again with the handle of a rake.

"Go away, Carlozo," I muttered. "I got no business with you." I curled up and rolled over, pulling a handful of hay up to my chin like a comfy quilt.

His voice was a mix of scorn and challenge. "You have sunk lower than I imagined possible. Filthy, haggard. How do you look at yourself in the mirror in the morning?"

"Simple. I sleep til noon. Now that you know my secret, hit the road and let me get on with my beauty regimen."

When he didn't reply, I closed my eyes and tried to quiet my agitated brain. I had just relaxed enough to doze off again, when a torrent of icy water hit me and shrank my skin as tight as a guy wire. "Hey, that bucket was my breakfast!" I jumped up, ready to box him on the ear hole a few times.

"Then here, dig in," he said and threw it at my midsection, knocking the wind out of me. A good thing, too: while time had forced Carlozo to start dying his hair and mustache the color of tar, I could see through his creamy satin shirt that his barrel chest and muscles were still hard as a sack of rocks. He could've pounded me into hash with biscuits on the side, but instead he did something worse: he made me do calisthenics. "Now pep up. Let's go. Hup hup. Start with jumping jacks."

Still dripping and addle-brained, I did as I was told and waved my arms like a plucked chicken trying to surrender. "What time is it anyway?"

"Six a.m. Best hour of the morning. I refuse to be associated with someone who would waste the day like you were doing. Now, side stretches, left five times, right five times, here we go." As I tried lifting my hand over my head, it felt like a hostler's whip had caught me in the armpit. Carlozo cared nanty for my cry of pain. "Don't be a baby, you'll thank me for this later."

"Not if you don't give me the chance to write my will," I moaned. "And what do you mean, 'associate with me'?"

2

"I need you to find someone for me," he said in a brisk tone. "Now, squat thrusts."

"Bah, impossible."

"You must do this job for me, I insist!"

"I'm not talking about that," I said. "Squat thrusts in these shoes?"

"You clowns and your ridiculous feet. All right then, windmills." We began flapping our arms.

"So, you need a detective. If you want to hire me, come back during office hours."

"Oh, and when is that?"

"Phone my office and find out."

"You have a phone?"

Despite the urge to throw up, I said, "Workin' on it."

"And while you 'work on it'," he mocked, "you operate out of this stable? The great Rex Koko, sleeping in a barn like an animal from the menagerie."

"It's not so bad," I said. "Daisy tried to turn this into a hothouse for growing orchids, but her visitors kept eating them."

"I don't doubt it," Carlozo said, "although the fresh greens might do you good. Pasty skin, stringy hair, flab everywhere...I shudder to think what you might be eating. Awful."

"Offal?"

"You agree?"

"Not with offal," I said.

"It's not awful?"

"Hell, it's terrible."

"Roots and beef blood," he said with conviction.

"Hey, I'm the guy who should be cursing here, Carlozo."

"What are you talking about? Now, run in place, hup hup. That's the best diet in the world: root vegetables and beef blood. Everything you need. Every day, roots and blood. If you'd watched your diet, you wouldn't be in agony now."

"No, if I'd locked my *door,* I wouldn't be . . . Aaaah! Oww!"

"This is just running in place! How hard can it be? Swing your arms a bit, pick your knees up . . ."

3

"Anything else?" I panted sarcastically.

He thought a moment. "Yes. You're not perspiring enough. Don't hold back, let yourself go."

"That's what I'd *been* doing," I protested, "and you showed up . . . and ruined it."

Carlozo snorted at me. "Your status is unique here in Top Town. Bottom of the ladder. Lowest of the low. A shambling *memento mori* . . ."

"Listen, smooth talker, I'm flopping . . . in Daisy's stall . . . while she visits relatives in Florida. Don't let . . . your dirty mind . . . make this something . . . it's not."

"Rumors fly around you like the flies in this stall," Carlozo prodded further. "And not just about the elephant, either. I want you for this job, Koko, because everyone hates you."

"I'm dying . . . from the irony," I gasped as the sweat poured down my 'paint. I was feeling pain in parts of my body I was sure I'd sold for pin money long ago. "What . . . where . . . who . . . ?"

He finally stopped, his hands on his hips, his heels planted firmly together. "I need you to find my wife, Adeline. She's missing."

Bent over double, I wheezed for air like a '25 Duesenburg. "Boots, missing? Next y'gonna tell me . . . the world revolves . . . around the sun?"

He glowered at me under his bushy, graying eyebrows. "I don't like the insinuation."

"Then you shouldn't have married it," I said. I might have been more diplomatic if I weren't in such pain, but I doubt it. "She gives you the air more often than a tire pump, then she always comes back. Just sit tight and leave your trailer unlocked, Bo Peep."

Carlozo clenched his jaw, making his mustache fidget. "I feel that will not work this time."

"Then why drag me into your mess?"

"Are you always so difficult with the people who want to hire you?" he asked.

"Probably not," I answered, "but some people make it easy. Go find her yourself."

"NO!" he yelled forcefully. "I am Reynaldo Carlozo! I will not be humiliated again. She is mine, and I want her back. And she needs to feel shame for what she has done to me, paraded through the streets and brought home where she belongs."

"All right, all right, I get your point, but I still don't . . ."

"Enough of this. *You* will be the one to bring her back. I will pay you $100 for the job. Here is ten to start."

He took out his roll and peeled off two Lincolns. He tossed them at me disdainfully, but I managed to catch them in midair. At least some of my reflexes were still intact. Ten bucks doesn't buy what it used to, except maybe the services of a broken-down joey who owes money to the moths in his grouchbag. "Okay, I'll do it. You've bought yourself a bird-dog."

Carlozo looked satisfied but not pleased. My taking the job may have validated his crummy opinion of me, but he was more saddened than satisfied. He was probably feeling sorry for himself that his personal situation had degenerated into this. The poor, misunderstood, tyrannical cuckold.

He raised his chin and explained, "I want you to bring her back so I can kill her."

CHAPTER 2

Strip Poker

Having said his piece, Carlozo styled, spun on his heel and walked out. Aching, sweaty and winded, I did a dead-drop backwards onto the hay. I'd taken a few beatings in my time, but this little exercise session was up there with the worst. At least I had some fold for my troubles. Now, my pounding head was asking, why did he want me to find his wife again?

Oh. Right. Well, maybe that was the turnips talking.

I pulled myself up eventually and began to collect my appurtenances. Daisy kept a neat and inviting stall, but it was time to move on. I didn't want her rep smeared when the other elephants on Bull Row began to gossip, which they were probably already doing. I dumped what few things I had into my kiester, locked it shut, and pulled it out into the street. In the morning sunlight colored with amber, I set the trunk on the curb and sat on it. I lit the last cigarette I'd mooched the night before, trying to figure out a next step that seemed worth taking.

Top Town was quiet at that hour, and Bull Row was in a quiet part of Top Town; the elephants commanded that much respect, so they got the prime real estate. About the only sound I could hear was the *swish-swish* of the bulls as they ate their breakfast. Their stalls looked clean and orderly from where I sat, freshly painted and lined up like rowhouses, with carved and gilded name plates hanging over each door. I'm sure a few were peering at me from inside as I sat there getting used to the freshness of the morning. Let 'em gawk, I didn't care. My hide had grown as thick as any pachyderm's over the past couple years.

I sat there in my sticky sweat, covered with chaff and hay like a dropped sucker. Despite the lingering agony in my body, I realized I owed a thank you to Carlozo. It's hard enough making a living as a detective, but it didn't help things to drop out of sight like I'd been doing. I'd tried to drink myself into obscurity, but I'm an inept drunk. I'm more likely to choke on a swizzle stick than die of cirrhosis. Maybe Carlozo's visit was timely, a blind-side slap to jolt me out of this mopery. Leave the exile act to Napoleon. A clown needs people, even when those people hate him.

If I was going to rejoin Top Town and mingle in not-so-polite company again, the first order of business was a nice boil-up. The next question was where to get it. Some joey in Clown Alley would probably be willing to lend me water and soap, but I didn't want to go over there just yet. Those guys are pals who've seen me at my worst and put up with a lot of grief defending my name when I didn't deserve it. I owed them something more like a grand entrance, clean, shaved and silly. I stood up and began to drag my battered kiester, with one other long-lost friend in mind.

Past Bull Row, the dusty streets were beginning to show signs of life, however slowly. At that moment Top Town and I shared something, a certain morning-after feeling of cheap hooch, too many cigarettes, and a hazy recollection of small favors and large regrets. This neglected corner of the city of Spaulding proper is packed with performers, troupers and hangers-on who've left the show, or had the show leave them. There were reasons aplenty for this—a bad injury, slowing reflexes, a loss of nerve, a battle with the bottle. Still, a lot of people around here keep working and practicing, dreaming of the day Big Bertha will give them that call, telling them to report to Sarasota to prep for next year's show. Whether this was from pluck or resilience or pure stupidity, I couldn't tell you. In circus folk, it's usually impossible to distinguish among those anyway.

Maybe the touring companies can turn up their noses, but the city here can't do without us. We provide Spaulding with diversions and spectacle every night of the week, a permanent midway, freak show and menagerie for their amusement and edification. Sailors and college boys come down to check out the exotic dancers, gawkers dawdle to stare at the freaks, young lovers stroll the midway and maybe win a stuffed animal at the shooting gallery. After the thrills, the drinks and the fights are over, all those elmers head home to a warm bed, and the kinkers are left with that uneasy pull to move on, but with no place to go.

I pulled my kiester behind me on the broken sidewalk, making what seemed like a tremendous racket, but no one stuck their heads out any windows to yell. Within four blocks, I could glimpse Griebling Avenue and its enviable collection of cooch shows. If a man couldn't find what he wanted here, it's because no one's thought of it yet—and believe me, they've thought of everything. The street's salacious reputation is immortalized in the old joke:

"Do you like Griebling?" asked a fine young fellow of a lady on the corner.

"Oh, yes, I do," said she, "but it's 50 bucks extra, and *you* pay for the harness."

I walked past Frenchy's Club, with its silly Eiffel Towers and dancing poodles painted all over the walls like a fun house. Further along, I admired the minarets and burlap palm trees of the Little Piece of Assyria. In its windows was a three-sheet describing the current show:

**25 of the World's most Captivating Beauties
dance for you in the manner of
Salome, Scheherazade and the other enticing
Sirens of History!
Experience the Temptations of the
Biblical Patriarchs!
Shocking! Instructional! Unbelievable!**

While I'm not a religious fellow, I made a note to check it out sometime.

Finally my destination came into view, the classiest joint on that classless street, the Club Bimbo. Its bulb-studded marquee glistened in the morning light, looking eager to get switched on again. Unlike some clubs, the Bimbo didn't even bother to list the current attractions outside; everybody knew you could get something there that you couldn't get at home, unless you happened to live with Caligula or Catherine the Great.

The owner and I went way back. Lotta Mudflaps had been some doll, curves in all the right places, times 20, plus a few in places you wouldn't expect. While she may have lost her title as "World's Daintiest Fat Lady," she still had plenty of energy and ambition. A jill running her own cooch show needed plenty of moxie, but that was Lotta all over. And over, and some more over there.

I tried the front door and was surprised to find it open. From the small red-carpeted lobby, I could hear someone inside the theater on piano playing a sad old song I couldn't place. I left my trunk by the vacant hat check window, tossed an imaginary tip in the bowl and turned down a hallway looking for Lotta's office. Coming in from the morning sunshine, I thought the place looked especially dark and filled with strange possibilities. From behind a flimsy wooden door came voices, one of which was instantly recognizable as Lotta's. She had a booming whoop that was the envy of every cowgirl on the Pecos. I'd been skulking in the hall no more than a minute, when chairs scraped and the door was opened. Out stepped a dapper old man with a trimmed white beard. He was dressed in a green wool suit, white shirt and a neat checked bowtie. In one hand he carried a Homburg hat and in the other a walking stick, which he needed because of a gimpy left leg. When he caught sight of me, he sized me with a steady eye. I retreated against the wall a bit to let him through.

Lotta followed him through the door. When she saw me, her expression was as over-the-top as something out of a silent movie, except it wasn't silent in the least. "*Rex!* Fer heaven's sake! What are yew doin' here?"

"Hey, Lotta, how ya doin'?"

"Fine as old wine, sugah," she said. "This *is* a surprise. Rex, may I introduce to yew a fine gentleman of the old school, Mr. T.C. Montgomery? We were just discussing a li'l business. Mr. Montgomery, this is my dear friend, the lord of laughter, Rex Koko."

Montgomery continued to size me up rather coolly, tipping his head back to take me in better. But I took a cool expression as a win these days. He extended his long, slender hand to me and said, "A pleasure, sir. I take it you are a friend from old performing days?"

"Yeah, me and Lotta go back a few years."

"He knew me back in my girlish youth, WOO-hoo-hoo-hooo," said Lotta.

Montgomery smiled, showing nests of wrinkles around his bright, moist eyes. It looked like life had been rough with him, but that he could give as good as he got. "Ah, the bonds that form between you troupers. The fraternity of showmen. Old friendships die hard, I daresay?"

"That's what I'm counting on," I said.

Lotta peered at me quickly, thinking maybe I came to sponge money instead of suds. It was only a fleeting look, but it made me feel guilty just the same. Montgomery chortled at my remark, and his dentures gave a short, rapid rattle, like the sound of half-dollars being stacked.

"Many people would envy that sense of camaraderie, Mr. Koko."

"You with the show, Montgomery?"

"More or less, but it was many moons ago, and the story's not worth telling," he confided. "In any event, I must run. Sir, madam, good day to you both." And with that, he settled his hat atop his coconut, rattled his choppers again, and left through the lobby.

"He's a slick old bird," I said, as we turned and walked the other way. "Sniffing around for some showgirls' phone numbers?"

"Rex, I'm surprised. Yew don't know T.C. Montgomery? He's one of the richest men in Top Town, and one of the nicest gentlemen. He doesn't go trawlin' fer showgirls. He doesn't need to."

"Then what's he doin' around here?"

"The better question," she said, smiling a little too directly at me, "is what are yew doin' around here? Y'been sneakin' around corners and shadows for so long around here, people were wonderin' had yew packed up and left town."

The two of us squeezed into Lotta's office, all red flocking and tasseled lampshades, and she wedged herself into the chair behind her desk. She was wearing a chemise of royal blue silk, patterned with subtle diamond shapes. Her brown hair was parted on the side and grew into a wavy nest behind each ear. The only jewelry she wore was a gold anklet (double-length) with a charm dangling from it. Once upon a time, she told me the charm was inscribed, "Heaven's Above."

"I've been in business all along," I stretched the truth a bit. "Maybe I kept my profile too low."

"A low profile's one thing, sugah," Lotta said, lighting a gasper, "but yew look like yew've been burrowing underground. I don't mind tellin' yew, Rex, Ah've been worried about yew. Disappearing for weeks on end. Ah don't even know how t'get a hold of yew if Ah need to."

"C'mon, girl, you know I always land on my feet. Kind of hard not to." For emphasis, I waved them in the air and accidentally knocked the shade off her desk lamp.

11

"Yeah, always the tough guy. Just don't forget yer friends around town."

"Hey, I came to see you, didn't I?"

"Mmmm-hmmm, Ah sure did notice," she purred looking at me sideways. "Maybe yew and Ah can start back where we left off, hmmmm? It's been a *long* time since Ah been with a man who knows how to treat me right!"

This was what I was afraid of. I returned her flirtation as breezily as I could. "Anything's possible, dollface, but you wouldn't want to be seen with me in my current state. Better that I have a boil-up before I start on my new job."

"*Job?*" she bellowed, shaking the glasses in the room. "Rex, yer on a *show* again?"

"Get serious, Lotta," I said. "Why would I want to be back on a show? My timing's off, everyone's stolen my best bits, and . . . well, the rest of it."

"What yew mean is," she said tiredly, "yew got another job as a dick."

"That's right. Someone hired me to find his wife and bring her back home."

"Who'd do a thing like that?" she asked.

"I don't think I should betray that confidence, Lotta."

"C'mon, Rex, it's a cinch to figure."

I waved her off. "I'm sorry. Professional code. My lips are zipped."

"It's Reynaldo Carlozo, right?"

"Wrong! It's Reynaldo Carlozo. Ha, smarty! So how about that boil-up?"

She smiled. "Ah just put in a nice shower by the dressing rooms. Yew'd be welcome to use it before the girls come in for the businessmen's luncheon."

"Lotta, you don't understand. I need to *soak*. I need to soak every bit of grime and grease outta me, every last drop of booze, every little stalk of hay, and then I need to soak some more. A shower ain't gonna cut the mustard."

"If y'want to be old-fashioned, go ahead," she said. "Ah can find yew a nice tub with hot water in the backyard . . . but only if Ah get to scrub yer back."

With her lewd, cartoonish grin, I couldn't tell if Lotta was kidding or not. When we first met, back with Reverend Underdown's Miracle Show, she was after me like a duck on a Junebug. One time, after a few too many rye squashes on a rained-out night in some backwater Illinois town, she and I had a little wrestling match. From what I can remember, I lost, both the match and the feeling in my legs. Ever since, she's always been ready to pipe up the band again. It flatters my ego but threatens my sacroiliac. Right now, I needed all the friends I could get. Lovers would have to wait.

"I still have my modesty, Lotta," I joked. "You'll have to wear a blindfold."

"Even better! That way, Ah can use my hands for feelin' around when Ah drop the soap." My face must've betrayed me, because she said, "Oh, come on, Rex honey. Don't start believing your own ballyhoo. Ah'm a businesswoman now, not some debutante lookin' to fill her dance card. Ah'll fix yew up, don't worry about that. It's good to see yew get back in the game, even as a detective."

"Time marches on, Lotta. I've got the footprints up my back to prove it. Now, what's up with that Montgomery gink?"

"What's with all the questions, punkin?" she asked sweetly but firmly. "Y'think having that big nose means yew can stick it in everyone's business? If yew have to know, Mr. Montgomery is going to invest in my club."

"Is the Bimbo in trouble? I always thought you were bringing in money pasties over g-string."

"Costs a lot to run a club these days," she said with resignation. "I've got to pay my dancers top dollar, or else they might jump ship for Fatima's or the Little Assyria. Then there's upkeep, liquor, patch . . ."

"You're already the most expensive joint on Griebling Street and you still can't make your nut?"

She heaved a great sigh and gave me a prickly look. "Lissen, y'wanna get clean, or y'wanna criticize how Ah do business?"

Smart move, Rex. Why don't you tell her to try a more flattering hairstyle while you're at it? "Sorry, old ton. I'll button my flap." To my left I saw a small table, on top of which sat a silver tray with a seltzer bottle, whiskey, bourbon, and a pair of tumblers from the bar. "Before the boil-up, how about a drink?"

"Now, Rex," she said worriedly, "don't y'think it's a mite early?"

Before she could finish, I grabbed the seltzer bottle and gave myself a hefty dousing of fizz water. In my mouth, up my nose, all over my coat. Lotta's concerned face relaxed and she gave up a good laugh.

"Ya-ha, good stuff!" I said, smacking my lips. I pointed the nozzle at her. "Join me? I hate to drink alone."

She shielded herself with her hands quickly. I pressed the lever and shot myself in the face again. It felt even better the second time. Recognizing one of my signature gags, Lotta whooped like a hyena on laughing gas.

CHAPTER 3

Shoot the Moon

In the Bimbo's back yard, Lotta set up an old washtub, filled it with buckets of hot water from the tap, and dutifully brought out teakettle after boiling teakettle to keep it comfy for me. Depending on where she poured, the water was either an invigorating flood of warmth or a threat to future generations of Kokos. Either way, it all felt good. I had a lot to sweat out, and this was the perfect way to do it.

Lotta hung a sheet on a line to give me a little privacy outside, but no one paid me much mind. On this fine morning, Top Town paid no attention to an old joey having a boil-up. Some of the girls from the club, however, kept finding excuses to come out in the yard, trying to check the old wives' tale about the size of a clown's feet and the rest of his anatomy, bless 'em.

Later Lotta brought out an old cane chair and threatened its continued existence as she sat and talked with me tubside. As I scrubbed my hide with a pig bristle brush, we cut up jackpots about the old days with the Underdown show, then with O'Heir's Parade of Oddities. We'd had some good times out on the road, stuff that only another kinker would appreciate.

"Ah sent yer duds out to be laundered, honey. Yer agent suit was in terrible shape."

"I know. Might have to get a new one made, once I grow a little hay."

"So, Carlozo's paying yew to bring his wife back home, huh? Shoot, Ah could do the job with a fishing line and a pair of pants."

"Oh? What do you know about her?"

"Ah've seen her a few times, heard a few stories. She's been waltzing around behind her husband's back for years. That's how she got her nickname, y'know—settin' her boots outside just anyone's trailer. She's already gone through almost all the flyers and catchers in town."

"Was Boots some kind of flyer, too?"

Lotta examined her nails nonchalantly, as if she weren't savoring every minute of this gossip. "Mmmm-hmmm. Apparently she was pretty good in her time. Trapeze, slack wire, iron jaw. Couldn't stick with one, I guess, so she played the whole card. Just like she does now. Last I heard, she was shackin' up with Berndt Bork."

"Yikes! Boiled cabbage for breakfast again?"

"WOO-hoo-hoo-hooo! No, ya big kidder, that ain't gas. Yew know Berndt Bork. He calls himself the Human Howitzer, parks his cannon over on Adler Street."

I nodded but kept my mouth shut. I had no idea who she was talking about. I must've been in the fog pretty long, if I hadn't heard of a kinker who explodes for a living. "You say she's over there now?"

"Can't tell ya fer sure. Last Ah heard, though, she was keepin' his barrel nice and polished."

"If that's the flap on the street, why does Carlozo need me to find her?"

"Beats me, honey," she said. "Yew wanna be a detective, better start askin' those questions yourself. But when yew catch up with Boots, give her a li'l message from me, wouldja, sugah?"

"What's that?" I said, soaping my toes.

"Tell her that if she ever tries to sink her claws into mah Rex, Ah'll tear off her pretty head and use it for a flower pot." The water in the tub suddenly felt chilly. I turned my head and looked in Lotta's steady gaze. She was three towns from kidding. "Now, if yew'll excuse me, Ah know some police who need paying off. Toodle-oo-hoo." With a mighty heave, Lotta got to her feet and waddled back inside the club.

It's nice to be wanted, I guess, if a little frightening.

Now, if even Lotta knew where Boots was camped out, what was stopping Carlozo from going to find his own wife? Couldn't he be bothered with the job? Had he been treated like royalty for so long that he got everything done through vassals and peasants? Maybe he didn't really want her back but for appearance's sake had to make a big spec of it. I was pretty sure he didn't really mean "kill" when he said "kill", just like I never mean "repay" or "apologize".

When the water in my tub finally got cold, I got out and toweled myself off. If I didn't feel quite human yet, at least I felt less like the scraps from an elephant's breakfast. Back inside the club, Lotta found me a place to shave, using one of the girls' dull razors. Staring back at me in the mirror over the sink was a well-worn, middle-aged joey, with an insolent Adam's apple, a crimson schnoz more long than round, and eyebrows arching high over exhausted brown eyes. My hair was still orange without a trace of gray, and without hope of ever covering more than the bottom third of my skull again. All in all, time had cut me some slack. I looked better than I felt, and I felt better than I had any right to.

Lotta had brought my agent suit to the dressing room, fresh from the cleaners. The overcoat was a shabby embarrassment, the yellow looking like dried mustard and the red circles dull and lifeless. It definitely needed replacing soon. But my little fedora still looked good, after spiffing it up with a toothbrush I found on the sink. I gave the same treatment to my shoes and walked to Lotta's office. She wasn't there, so I helped myself to a cup of coffee and a couple biscuits from her secret larder, then started off.

Out in the hazy sunshine, I pointed my 42s down Griebling toward Adler. Despite feeling clean, shaved and fed, I still had a vaporous twinge of misgiving. You'd think I'd be used to this feeling by now, but here it was again. The streets of Top Town hadn't changed nor, I was guessing, had people's attitudes. But short of capturing Hitler single-handedly, there wasn't much I could do about it. Half the voices in my head were telling me to go back to Daisy's stall and curl up until dark. The other half kept saying, "Pratfall, pratfall! Come on, Rex, trip on something! Yay! Big laughs!"

I really need to have a word soon with the voices in my head.

As I turned left on Grimaldi Street—Top Town's main street, if you could say it had one—a pungent aroma told me I was getting near the Monkey Hostel. In warm weather, when the windows are open, anyone walking by is guaranteed a nasty barrage from the hostel's residents, so I grabbed the lid of a nearby ashcan and used it as a shield. *Ptannng! Ptannng!* The monks made two direct hits, but other than that I came out okay.

I threw my shield aside and, not watching where I was going, bumped into something large and solid. In front of me on the side-walk, wearing a dirty brown canvas jacket and a battered cap, stood Missouri Redd, one of the Redd Brothers, a gang of Top Town roustabouts always looking for a clem. (They were actually all half-brothers whose father, while traveling with troupes over the years, littered the country with bastard red-headed whelps all the way up into Canada.) I'd never dealt with Missouri, but he had advance as the Redd with the shortest fuse and the thickest skull.

"Watch where yer goin', clown," he growled through yellow teeth.

"My mistake, brother. Just trying to dodge some simian valentines."

Answering him seemed to make him angrier. "What th' hell are you talkin'?" he said, his complexion like bad corned beef. "I don't want no explanation from you, I want you outta my way."

"I'll get right on that, pal, as soon as you quit standing on my feet."

"Y'know somethin', you got a smart mouth. It's gonna get you in trouble someday."

Before I knew it, Missouri Redd grabbed me and tossed me back in front of the Monkey Hostel. I tripped over my own feet and sprawled on the sidewalk. His mean, piggy eyes gleamed with poisonous joy as I was pelted with monkey muck from the open windows. The monkeys screeched and hooted, for all I know keeping score of the bulls-eyes. I picked myself up and ran into the street, out of reach of the roustabout, and kept on running. The inbred moron just watched with intense satisfaction, so nasty that his mirth could only sneak out of his mouth in little gasps.

Lucky for me, no crowd was around to witness my humiliation. Just a venomous goon weaned on stumpwater and axle grease and two dozen monkeys screeching in satisfaction. When I stopped running, I looked at my formerly clean agent suit. The muck made a few small stains that a little water could daub out, but that pug left two black hand prints on my chest when he pushed me. Some kind of grease or oil, and it would be a helluva time getting it out. I got my hankie out of my pocket and wiped off my coat as I walked. I'd send my cleaning bill to Missouri Redd if I knew which boxcar he was sleeping under.

I turned down Adler Street, looking for Bork's. I passed a grocery store, a closed mitt camp, a guess-your-weight booth, and a liquor store, then turned a bend and saw the silver barrel of a cannon hanging 15 feet over the sidewalk. Unless some admiral had dry-docked his battleship here, it looked like I'd found the Human Howitzer. A high plank fence surrounded the lot, but the door was unlocked, so I pushed my way in.

The lot had that "lived-in" look, like an Army motor pool had lived in it for the better part of a decade. Metal drums were scattered around as if by some heavy-industry Easter bunny, plus crates, boilers, tires and scrap metal. Puddles of mud, oil and who knew what else made walking dangerous. And amid all this dismal grime stood a firm-jawed blonde man in a spotless silver jumpsuit, staring off into the distance, looking like a Viking captain at the helm of his rowboat.

He didn't notice when I entered the yard. I cleared my throat a few times and kicked a stray can or two, but our intrepid hero still stared into the distance, his crash helmet tucked under his arm. When I got close enough to tap him on his silver shoulder, I managed to scare him silly.

"Sorry about that," I said. "You Berndt Bork?"

"I didn't hear you come up," he said. "Then again, my hearing ain't what it used to be."

"Am I interrupting practice?"

"Yep. Gotta get back on the road soon, earn some spread. With our boys winning in Europe now, it won't be long before people will be able to handle an act like mine again. For a while, people just didn't like a guy with a German name driving around with a big cannon."

Sounded like a cheap rationalization to me—stage names are as common as head lice among kinkers—but I wasn't this guy's confessor. "I'm looking for someone, Addie Carlozo. She been around here?"

His face turned suspicious. "And who the hell are you, barging onto a guy's lot and asking questions?"

"Just a joey doing a favor for someone. I ain't looking for trouble."

"Yeah, I don't know you from Adam."

"Name's Rex Koko. Tell you what. You just answer my questions, and I'll help you out, Buck Rogers. I'll go over there and be your net-sitter for a while, as you practice your . . . jumps? Shoots? Bangs? Whatever you call 'em, your *whoooshes* through the air."

Bork sighed and looked off in the distance again. I don't know much about this kind of act, but I thought his whole cannon apparatus was mighty impressive. Resting on the flat bed of a long-haul truck, it was shiny as a newlywed's frying pan and studded with a couple thousand rivets. The truck was up on wooden blocks, and held down against recoil with ropes and stakes like Gulliver on a beach vacation. From the look of it, Bork could slap on the wheels and drive his peashooter to any circus or county fair he wanted. But after sitting for a couple years, it was going to be that much harder for man and machine to hit the road again.

"All right, clown, I'll level with you. Boots was here for about a week. Then last Sunday she disappears. No note, nothing. Easy come, easy go."

"Meaning . . ."

"Meaning, one day she just showed up at my door, ready to bunk up. I'd met her once or twice, but we barely knew each other, and she showed up here like she was expectin' a surprise party or somethin'."

"Where'd she go?"

"Search me. I wasn't going to follow her. She was a looker, but from the start I knew she wasn't going to stick around. She had those kind of eyes that were always searching for the next chump to latch on to."

"You knew she was married."

"Sure, I knew it. Said her old man wasn't doing it for her any-more, since he didn't hit the trapeze. Things were pretty ugly at home. She said he was always ready to hit her."

"Did he?"

"Don't know. She had such a mouth on her, there were times I thought of hitting her myself. Don't get me wrong, that's not my style. But she was one mouthy, demanding broad. Helluva temper, too."

"Do you know her husband?"

"Not really. Just the name."

"And you got no idea of where she went?"

"No. I'm telling you, that's all I know. Now, I'd like to get in one more flight before lunch. You gonna net-sit for me? Head that way."

Bork strapped on his reinforced aviator's cap and climbed up the ladder near the opening of the cannon. With a well practiced move, he grabbed the metal handle on top of the barrel, lifted himself up and slid himself in feet first, slick as a wiener in a bun. Satisfied that everything was OK, he gave me a thumbs up and disappeared inside. I started to walk down the lot to where his safety net was strung, stepping carefully among all the puddles and debris, which were such a contrast to the sleek sheen of Bork himself and all his gear. Maybe he galvanized himself every night before he went to bed.

Behind me I heard a crack, then a massive thump that made the ground shake. Turning around, I saw something was screwy. From where I was, it looked like Bork's truck and cannon had fallen backward, off its blocks. The barrel was no longer aimed straight above me, but instead was pointing up and off to the east. The instant I thought of running back to do something—anything—to help Bork, the cannon fired. Whistling in an eerie way, the Human Howitzer flew by so quickly the expression on his face was a blur. All I could see was the flash of the sun off his goggles before he passed from sight, headed for an unpleasant rendezvous with something solid a couple of streets over.

CHAPTER 4

Poker Face

By the time I made it over to Nock Street, you didn't need a bloodhound to tell where Bork had landed. People were dribbling out of the doors of all the nautch joints there, and along with the loiterers and passersby, were converging on a black sedan stopped in the middle of the street. When I got within 30 feet, I spotted Bork's body in its silver wrappings lying in front of the car. You couldn't mistake him for a shiny hood ornament anymore.

There's something mesmerizing about a dead body. Bork was obviously past help, but that didn't stop more and more gawkers from crowding around, as half-naked people leaned out of the building windows, shouting questions. I was pulled into it too, though God knows I don't need to see any more stiffs in my life. Everyone heads south sometime, whether with a bang or a whimper, but still we stare and stare, like it's just some gag and the body's going to jump up and yell "April Fool," or tell us how the crowded lines along the banks of the River Styx made him throw up his hands and come back.

I stared with the rest of the chumps until a thick, acrid gravy started climbing up my throat and my hands and feet felt frostbitten. The whispers and chatter seemed to grow louder. Nobody was looking at me, but I needed to hide just the same. By the time a couple of dark-suited flatties pushed their way through the crowd and told everyone to move along, I didn't need to be asked twice. I took off running and was halfway down Jacobs Avenue before I got the feeling in my toes back.

I leaned on a bench and tried to calm down. Daredevils live on the edge of danger, I reminded myself. They work to cheat Death time after time, but eventually Death catches on to the grift. Happens all the time. Well, maybe not *all* the time, or else you'd have a whole lot more world premieres and fewer encores. But why'd it have to happen when I was around? Why the hell did Carlozo have to send me out on this wild Boots chase? Word about Bork would get around Top Town soon enough. Lotta knew I was headed to see him, and others probably saw me walk into his back lot. I had to find Carlozo, maybe set up some kind of alibi.

How's that for colossal ego? Some poor kinker's lying dead in the street, not even cold yet, and all I can think about is saving my own pasty hide? In a word, yep.

Carlozo might give me an alibi, or he might give me the toe of his boot. One thing he hadn't given me yet was his address or phone number. Did we have any mutual friends or acquaintances? That's a weak laugh. Clowns and flyers weren't exactly chummy as a rule. So where might flyers be hanging out in the middle of the day? One location stood out in my mind, so I hightailed it back up to Griebling Street.

The bars around Top Town—the local bars, anyway—have very particular clienteles. Everyone has his own place to water his tonsils, and is expected to stay there. The joeys have the Banana Peel, the windjammers hang out at Merle's, the freaks frequent Pip & Flip's. And the flyers, catchers and wire-walkers hold court at Jimmy's Hi-Wire. It was early afternoon by now, so the place should've been open. I was going to have to try my luck there.

The front door of Jimmy's was covered in black leather with one of those porthole windows in the middle. From the outside the place looked sleek and well oiled, like a building that dreamed of being a limousine. I pushed the door open, squinting to adjust my eyes to the light. In the middle of the day, you'd expect a regular saloon to be darker inside than the bright, sunlit street, but Jimmy's was not a regular saloon. Instead of lights hanging from the ceiling and shining down, Jimmy's Hi-Wire had its lights installed under heavy glass on the floor, pointing up. This shot a harsh glare onto the customers, whose heavy shadows loomed monstrously on the ceiling and walls. And since the source of the light was near the customers, their shadows zipped around the upper corners with unreal speed. The cigarette smoke shone bright and clean like silk ribbons and all the glasses sparkled like fine crystal. People's faces, however, were garish and frightening, like when you shine a flashlight under your face to tell ghost stories.

The front door lets you into the middle of the room, with the bar to your left side and tables and booths to the right. In the middle of the room were cables, ropes, nets, ladders and other exotic apparatus, strung up like a giant cat's cradle. Wire-walking, Planges, Roman rings, iron jaw tricks—you name it, if you wanted to fly through the air after getting a snootful, Jimmy's had the rigging in place. Right now, things were quiet, but when the joint was jumping, more than a few flyers probably went airborne to win bets, impress girls, or shake the earth's mud off their feet and live in the clouds for a while, which is all these guys yearned for anyway. You know what it's like to talk to people who really want to be somewhere else, or just need to go to the donniker real bad? The restless feet, the shifty eyes, the shoulders poised to turn and leave? Multiply that by a hundred or so, and that's what it's like talking to a flyer.

The Hi-Wire wasn't very busy at this time of day. The tables were unoccupied, and maybe 10 ginks or so were hanging around the bar. I didn't see Carlozo anywhere, but since I'd already come this far, I decided to push my luck. Girding up my loins, I walked into the place like a regular. Unfortunately, it'd been years since my loins had suffered such treatment. The sharp pain made me miss a few stairs, and I did a dead drop face-first to the floor. So much for looking like one of the regulars.

With as little noise as I could muster, I picked myself up from the floor. The stares from the barflies should've made me turn around and hit the road, but I smiled and waved slightly, assuring everyone I was okay and pointing to the back like I just needed to retrieve a lost umbrella. Score a point for fear masquerading as brass—I made it around the corner with my heart racing and burst through the first door I found. I held my ear to the door to listen for anyone following me.

"Hey, ace," sang a man's voice, "doesn't a closed door mean anything anymore?"

I nearly jumped out of my 42s. Turning around, I found myself in a nicely furnished office, with leather chairs, filing cabinets and a handsome, muscular man with sandy hair standing behind a desk. His mood was pleasant, despite the fact that I had interrupted him while he was shaving his armpits.

"Sorry," I stammered, "I was just um . . . ah . . . er . . ."

"You were just 'um-ah-er,'" he mimicked. "That's good. I'd hate to think you just came bouncing around my club for some cheap laughs."

"I'm . . . looking for someone."

"Ain't we all?" he said, as he calmly wiped the lather from his chest with a towel and powdered his torso briskly with a palm full of talcum. He then slipped on his sleeveless undershirt and a crisp maroon shirt that had been hanging on a nearby rack. The guy was six foot four or five, almost as stacked as Carlozo, but 20 years younger. From a radio someplace, Strauss' "Blue Danube" played very softly. Just like at Lotta's place, I couldn't tell if I was in a nightclub or a boudoir. At least at the Bimbo, I had a little more to look at. "Oh, ain't we all? Me, I'm looking for a clever accountant, and a woman who won't kiss and tell."

"Sorry to interrupt your shaving," I said.

"I didn't cut myself, so all's forgiven," he said with a charming smile. "Besides, we're all used to close quarters, eh? Even after retiring. What's your name, bigshoe?" I told him. He looked into the mirror hanging on the wall and smoothed the pomade in his hair with his hand. "Glad to meet you. I'm Jimmy Plummett. The Hi-Wire is my place. So unless I'm the fella you're looking for . . ."

"Well, really, I've got business with Reynaldo Carlozo."

Plummett blew a squeaky laugh through his nose like the sound of corduroy rubbing together. "That's a hot one. Well, too bad. Even if I believed you, he isn't here. Now, ace, I'm gonna ask you to leave. I like a clown act as much as the next guy, but my customers, you can understand . . ."

He came around the desk to me, but I moved around to the other side. Framed glossy photos were hung all over the wall, and gave me an idea for stalling my eviction. "Wait a sec, you're THE Jimmy Plummett?" I asked, taking great interest in the pictures. "Wow! Wait til I tell the guys I saw you shaving your nipples!"

The egotist in him nearly took the bait. "Nice try," he said, as he continued to chase me.

"Jimmy Plummett, that name's known all over, right? You've probably been on shows all over the world." I began to point to pictures and name any circus that popped into my head, all the time walking around the desk faster. "You've flown with the biggest, I bet." I whistled loudly in admiration.

Suddenly Jimmy stopped chasing me with a terrified look. I thought he'd had a stroke or something, until he leaned over to his desk and knocked on the wood surface. Superstitions dog some kinkers, just like actors and other performers, and whistling backstage is a huge no-no. Some of the worst of these scaredy-cats are the flyers.

"Now, I'm telling you again, ace, cut out the antics and beat it." Jimmy came at me with more fury in his eyes.

"I've always wondered," I said, as we continued round his desk, "do you guys ever get sick of that 'Daring Young Man' song? I've sure had *my* fill of it over the years." Just as Jimmy was about to touch me, I whistled a snatch of the old tune. He froze again, turned too quickly to find some oak to choke, and tripped on a corner of the carpet. I didn't wait to see him crash into the furniture, but instead escaped through the door and into the bar. But there in the garish lighting, who do I spy hoisting himself onto a barstool but my client, looking more bleary-eyed than he had at six in the morning.

"Hey Carlozo! Fancy running into you. We need to talk . . . y'know, haha . . . about this morning." He turned and looked at me like I was a beagle talking Egyptian, then faced the bar again. "Listen, I did like you said to do, but somebody did something to somebody else somewhere, and now I need you to say I didn't do what it was you said I had to do, even though I did it like you said to."

Plummett was coming out of his office now in great limping strides. "Carlozo, listen, I need an alibi," I said, more insistently. "I was with you all morning, right? Teaching orphans to bowl? Wrapping bandages for the Red Cross? Canning peaches?" Still no response, as Jimmy lifted me by the collar, breathing heavy. "Carlozo! A little help here!"

"Back to Clown Alley with you," sneered Jimmy, as another flyer grabbed my arm to help.

"Somebody's dead!" I yelled in Jimmy's face. He and the other guy stopped for a minute. "A flyer, a daredevil . . . Berndt Bork! He's dead! He got shot too far and hit heavy traffic on Nock Street."

Jimmy stuck his nose two inches from mine. "Listen, you think I don't know who you are? Huh? If Berndt Bork's dead, you probably had something to do with it. You're worse than bad luck, Koko. You're practically the Grim Reaper. Now you get out of my club before you cause a disaster in here!"

When Jimmy said this, every flyer in the place gasped and did something to repel the evil eye—signed the cross, spit over his shoulder, made wiggly motions under his chin with his fingers.

"Carlozo! What's the matter with you?"

"You leave him out of it," Jimmy said as I was picked up and carried away. Somebody opened the front door for us. "And stay away from here!" They tossed me out hard enough that I sailed eight feet and hit the lamppost on the curb face first.

If you want my opinion, flying ain't all it's cracked up to be.

CHAPTER 5

Jokers Wild

I lay stretched out on the sidewalk in front of the Hi-Wire, gazing blearily at the impression my face had made in the lamppost. A fair likeness, and certainly no worse than the impression I'd made inside the bar.

"Hey Rex! What's with the gong sound? Chinatown's a couple blocks thataway!"

Even with the bells still ringing in my head, that falsetto was familiar. Loopy, warbling, on the brink of a giddy fit. As I swerved my newly fragile head around, the buildings and blue sky swooped and swayed. Then, the smiling mug of my old pal Bingo came into focus. As embarrassing as my present position was, he'd seen me in worse, and had never been anything but true blue. And discreet. And cackling like a lunatic.

"What're ya doin', goin' into a joint like Jimmy's for?" he asked as he helped me up on my feet and dusted me off with a little whisk broom he pulled out of thin air. "I always knew you were crazy, but I didn't know you were stupid."

I shook my head to try and make the world less slippery, with little success. "Ah, I just had a taste for a cocktail, and

I figured if anybody knew how to make a good highball...."

"Highba- Oooh hoooo hooo hoooo! *High*ball! Aw, Rex, you ain't lost it. If you're looking for a little eel juice, pally, come on with me. I was just headed down to the Banana Peel. Lemme buy ya some fresh squeezin's."

"It's a nice offer, Bingo, but . . . ah . . ."

"Come on, the walk will do you good, and the booze will do you better. Hey, lemme tell ya! I just saw the craziest thing. I was just over on Nock Street, getting my weekly canasta lesson from Maggie and Simone . . ."

"Come on, Bingo, three-handed canasta?"

"Frankly, I lost track of how many hands were working. Ohh hooo hooooo! Yowza! So, I'm giving the girls a breather and having a smoke by the window, when what do you think I saw?"

"Your mother in the nautch joint across the way?"

"No, you idiot!" he barked. "Mom has Mondays off. Anyhoo, I'm lookin' out and I see this silver blur come zooming out of the sky. Whoooosh! I can't tell what it is until it stops. And boy, does it stop, BAM! Right into the grill of a DeSoto. And I see that it's a guy. It's some kind of human cannonball."

"Wow, must be a first for that," I said, feeling evasive and guilty.

"So this cannonball is now at liberty, permanent-like. Probably not so easy to eat when your head's been knocked into your chest. But here's the best part: the car this cannonball hit, y'know who it belongs to? Take a wild guess."

"Harry Truman."

"No, but you're close. The car belonged to Mayor Brody! In broad daylight, this guy smacks right into the mayor of Spaulding. Hoo hoooo!"

"Mayor Brody? Cripes, what the hell's *he* doin' down in Top Town?"

"If he's on Nock Street, he ain't gettin' a snow cone, that's fer sure. This could bring some serious heat down here, I bet. Scandal, reporters, police, the works. Could liven things up a bit. Look out, Rex!" Just as I was about to set foot into Kay Street, Bingo grabbed my collar and choked me with a yank backward. A second later, a couple of bareback riders came galloping past the corner inches from the two of us. "Jeez, open yer eyes. If you can't *see* that you're near the Hippodrome, you should at least be able to *smell* it."

"My mind's somewhere else, Bingo."

"It'll be all over the pavement if you ain't careful, pally."

Bingo was more on target than he knew. The last thing I, or anyone else in Top Town, needed was a bunch of fuzz around making life difficult. Normally a killing down here doesn't get any attention. If Bork had died without hitting the car of someone important, the cops would hardly bother to sweep up the pieces. Now they could gum up the works plenty. If I wanted to figure out what happened, I'd have to stay close to things but not too close, or else the bulls would try to close the case down around my ears and I'd get to have my mail forwarded upstate. I needed to stay out of the spotlight and still find an alibi for the afternoon.

"Come on, Bingo, I've changed my mind. I need to hoist a couple. Let's get to the Peel before Blinky does his trick with the olives."

"Yeah, the martinis never taste quite kosher after that."

The Banana Peel isn't easy to find, even after you've been there a few times. Hard to believe about a shack painted canary yellow and sour-apple green, but it's the truth. If you try and follow any set of directions to go there, you'll get lost and probably end up knee-deep in the harbor. But get the directions wrong, and you'll slide right in the front door.

Why was this our oasis in Top Town? Well, in some taverns, you leave the troubles of the world at the front door. At the Banana Peel, you bring the troubles of the world right inside with you, give it a place at the bar, and pour oatmeal down its pants. If Sigmund Freud were to happen by and try to figure out how Banana Peel ticks, he'd never make it out alive. But this much is certain: he'd die with a smile on his face.

Bingo and I pushed through the swinging double doors and entered the bar. It was dark inside, reeking of cigarettes and cream pies. As usual, the place looked like a cyclone had taken out its frustrations on it. Chairs and tables were piled up in crazy, suggestive, inexplicable ways. One table had six chairs piled one on top of another all the way to the ceiling, on top of which was an icebox with someone's legs hanging out. A twisted bicycle was lying near a broken teeterboard, there was moaning coming out of an old pickle barrel, and a goat I'd never seen before was peeling off strips of wallpaper for a snack. I'd lost count of how many times I'd embarrassed myself here over the years, how many ridiculous fistfights, how many bad spit takes. Thankfully, clowns' memories are short, and can be wiped completely by a good belly laugh. Sometimes I feel like the only joey around who can hold a grudge or nurse a regret.

About a dozen zanies were getting oiled up around the bar on the right-hand side. I recognized them all: Goose, Skeets, Chigger, Paulie Punchinello, Mr. Whoops, and the rest of them. They looked up a little when we entered, but kept up their conversations in low mumbles and muted honks.

"Hey fellas," keened Bingo as we came up, "make way for the headliners. A round of drinks on me!"

Down washed a cascade from everyone around us, of rum, red-eye, rotgut, rob roys, Roy Rogers and plain old crappy beer, some of it still in the bottle. Bingo sputtered and smacked his lips contentedly. "Ahhhh, *that* hit the spot! A couple of times over, even." He waved the bartender over. "Hey, Sid . . ."

"Stan."

"Stan, hand me a towel and then a beer."

Sid pulled Bingo and me a draft, as well as drinks for the rest of the crowd. I sipped it a little, but was too keyed up to enjoy it. I let Bingo do most of the talking, which isn't hard to do. He was nattering on about his rock-solid information that Eleanor Roosevelt had a secret, unquenchable appetite for clowns, when I felt a large presence looming behind me. Bingo stopped talking and stared steadily over my shoulder, giving me an extra jigger of the willies. I sipped my beer one last time and turned on my stool. There stood Happy Jingles, all six feet and 240 pounds of him.

He scratched the stubble on his chin with a gloved hand, as if suspicious of his good luck. "So, Koko," he said with a voice like wet gravel, "I'm surprised to see you around here again."

"Oh, Happy?" I said. "Why's that?"

"The last time you showed up here, you borrowed 75 bucks from me, and since then, I ain't seen any trace of it, or you."

I had no recollection of any such mooch, which didn't mean it didn't happen, or that Happy wasn't making it up just to be a clod. This joey had more chips on his shoulder than a sloppy lumberjack. It was usually best just to give him a lot of room and watch your back. "Yeah, well, I've been out of circulation," I said, "and if I did borrow that much, you'll have to wait . . ."

"'If'? There's no 'if' about it! You borrowed 75 bucks from me and I want it now."

Bingo butted in: "Listen, Sappy, every time you open your mouth, something stupid falls out. Do us all a favor and buzz off."

"Shut it, Bingo. Rex is a big boy. He can stand up for himself. He knows what he did, and he can pay it back."

The whole place fell silent, waiting to see how this was going to end. Happy Jingles rocked on his heels confidently, his left hand fingering the edge of his frilly collar. By this point, it didn't matter whether he was setting me up or not. He'd dropped the wallet, so it was up to me to reach down for it and see what happened next.

"Happy, Happy, Happy," I said, sliding off my stool, "I'm glad you brought this to my attention."

"Uh-huh," he said eagerly.

"And I'd be glad, my old friend, to resolve this situation, but first I have a question. If I did borrow this sum of moolah, as you assert, where in fact did I spend it?"

"Beats me," he shrugged.

"'Beats you'? 'Beats you'? You fork over 75 smackers and you have no idea where it went? Was it wine? Women? Helium? Where did it go?"

"I got no idea."

"'I got no idea'," I mocked. "Do you expect us to believe that? Do you expect us to believe you'd toss away that much skejeema not even knowing where it was going? You'd have us believe you're some kind of Daddy Warbucks, that you light your cigars with ten dollar bills? Is that what you're saying, Mr. Rockefeller?"

"No, no, I'm not like that . . ."

"No, I would think not," I continued in my best interlocutor voice, "in fact, we haven't determined where you got the money in the first place. These 75 clams you claim is yours— how do we know where *you* got it?"

"Yeah!" said Bingo and a few others caught up in the argument.

"Hey, I didn't do . . . ," Happy protested.

"As if we can believe anything you say by now. All right, where'd you glom that money, Happy? Where'd you steal the 75 dollars?"

"I . . . I don't know . . . I," he stammered in tearful confusion. "It all happened so fast . . ."

"We oughta run you outta Top Town on a rail! Thief! Marauder! Picaroon!"

"Wait a minute!" My courtroom performance was interrupted by the high, girlish voice of Bunzie, a drag clown who was a regular fixture around town. "Wait just a cotton-pickin' minute!" he said, pushing his ridiculous knockers between us and batting his sticky eyelashes. "This all started about *you* borrowing the dough."

This brought Happy Jingles back to his senses. "Yeah . . . yeah . . . what *about* it, Koko? Where's my 75 bucks?"

Every eye in the place was on me. Sid the bartender wisely ducked out of sight. "Seventy-five bucks?" I asked. "Seventy-five bucks?"

"Yeah, where's my 75 *bucks?*"

I shrugged my shoulders. "Haven't got it."

Shrieks of laughter flooded the room. I'd lost him, had him, lost him again—and the joeys ate it up. Slaps on the bar, bent-over guffaws, whoops raised to the ceiling—everybody loved it. Everybody but Happy Jingles. It looked like I really *did* owe him the money. He leaned back to take a swing at me, but I ducked. He kept spinning around and slapped Bunzie hard. His effeminate defender flew backwards, feet in the air, and smashed a table on the way down.

From out of nowhere someone threw a pie, then another. The shrieks and cackles got louder as the slapsticks and hammers got passed around. Paulie Punchinello ran to the haggard piano in the corner and started banging out an off-key "Clown Alley Sally."

I wanna get pally with Clown Alley Sally.
Who's been in her Big Top
The number is too big to tally,
Oh, what a gally, that Clown Alley Sally,
She's got a hotter trailer
Than the comet of old Mister Halley . . .

More pies, seltzer, rubber balls, even a baby pig went flying. Skeets found a bucket of whitewash and a long-handled mop and was busy soaping up the floor under everyone. Somebody snuck up behind me and knocked me down with an Indian club. I looked up from the floor and saw it was Happy Jingles. But the gleam in his eye wasn't anger or revenge. It was joy, it was chaos, good old clown chaos. He shrieked at me and I howled back, then I yanked his pants down to his ankles and knocked him backwards into some chairs. He laughed like a maniac the entire time.

And it went on and on, for God knows how long, this mayhem. This glorious, heavenly pandemonium. I'd been away from this scene and away from these idiots for too long, and God help me but I missed it. It did me more good than a hundred boil-ups.

CHAPTER 6

Up the Ante

A couple hours later, the joeys all ran out of laughing gas. The only sounds you could hear in the Banana Peel were gaspings for air, the spray of water from the broken sink in the bathroom, and the goat asking to be let outside. Poor old Sid emerged from beneath the bar. The long-suffering bartender took off his catcher's mask, surveyed the damage, and went into the back to get a mop and a shovel.

I ended up in the front corner by the door, a hat rack up the back of my coat and my hand stuck in a spittoon. While I had a few bumps and bruises, the biggest pains came from my laugh-torn ribcage. I know some joeys who are boozers, some who prefer to dance with men, some who cheat on their wives and their ration cards, but I never met one who could keep himself out of a full-scale clown blow-out like the ones we have at the Peel. We're like bears in heat that way, and any unsuspecting flatties better get out of the way. Come to think of it, the bears ought to watch out for themselves, too.

A pile of rubbish next to me moved. Bingo emerged from beneath it, wearing a dazed expression and a toilet seat for a collar. "Hoooooboy," he exhaled quietly, "now *that's* what I call a punchline."

"Man, Bingo, my sides are killing me. I was fit to choke to death when you did your impersonation of Hitler's dog."

"C'mon Rex, that was nothin'. You been away too long, that's all. Belly on up to the bar and let's do the old 'Mae West Meets a Pygmy' bit."

"Thanks, pal, but I've got to get going" I said, although he and I could barely move. "Can you help get this cookie jar off my hand?"

"What's with you anyway, Rex?" said Bingo, sounding sore. "You act like you've got to be somewheres, but where the hell could that be?"

"Didn't I tell you? I've got a job."

"In a pig's eye! Who'd want to hire a washed-up, paranoid, useless bum like you? No offense."

"None taken. I'm supposed to help a husband find his wife."

"Hey, that's a switcheroo. *I'm* always finding wives who've run out on their husbands. Oooohoohoohoooo!" This was no three-sheeting. Bingo had visited more women in bed than the tooth fairy.

"Maybe you can help me, then. You know Addie Carlozo?"

"Boots Carlozo? Sure, we been around the circuit a few times."

"You know where she is now?"

"Last I heard, she was shacking up with a kinker over on Mardo Street. Guy named Flying Fleming. Does a high dive act. She's the skirt you're supposed to bring in? Oohoooo, good luck, pally. She's one tough creampuff. She dislocated my hip once, and we were only shakin' hands."

"I tell ya, every time I mention her name, people practically want to spit. Is she really that much trouble?"

"Boots has some bad advance," said Bingo, "but she's not the kind to give a hoot. Some people even say she's a black widow. But if she is, then she stinks at her guzintas, 'cuz she ain't a whole lot richer for the effort."

"She sounds like a piece of work," I said, surprising myself with the admiration in my voice.

"Lemme tell ya, she could put air in anyone's balloon. Even yours, pally. So, you're back to being a detective, huh? Hooo haaaah! The private dick, and all like that. Didya ever bother to apply for that license?"

"Nah. The way I look at it, Bingo, if you've got a driver's license and you crack up a car, that means you're a bad driver. If you don't have a license and you crack up a car, that means you're just an idiot."

Bingo thought this over a minute. "I see your point, pally," he finally said. "Wear your hat so no one else will notice."

Next to us, the front door opened, but whoever it was didn't come in. He was probably wondering whether this gin mill was about to fall in on its foundations. Slowly, the hesitant head of Reynaldo Carlozo came into view. He didn't see Bingo and me in our piles of junk.

"Close the door!" I shouted. "You're lettin' fresh air in."

Carlozo nearly jumped out of his flimsy, fancy shoes. Bingo started laughing in his inimitable cuckoo way. The color rose in Carlozo's face, but he managed to speak calmly. "Mr. Koko, may I speak with you outside for a moment?"

"As you can see, Mr. Carlozo, affairs have me slightly tangled up right now. May I inquire as to the nature of your visit?"

He paused and said, "I'd rather talk about it outside."

"All right, play your little game. I'll be out in a bit." He left, with a lingering stare at the wreckage inside the bar. I took my sweet time leaving—not that I had a lot of choice, weighted down with various pieces of furniture. Once I was on my feet again, I strolled back to the bar and had a swallow of beer from an unbroken schooner. Carlozo was due for a taste of his own medicine, I thought. Let him cool his heels outside of the clown bar and see how he likes the stares.

When I got outside, I was surprised to find the afternoon was almost over. Carlozo was pacing back and forth, smoking like a train behind schedule. When he saw me, he threw down the butt and stormed over.

"What's the big idea, keeping me hanging around like this?"

"Sorry, but you can imagine, Happy Hour at the Banana Peel is pretty intense."

"Why, you imbecile . . ." He made a motion like he was going to strangle me, but I slapped his hands to the side.

"Save it, Carlozo. You left me flapping in the wind like Old Glory up at Jimmy's, looked me straight in the puss and pretended you didn't know me. What the hell was that all about?"

"I could never acknowledge . . ."

"Why'd you hire me, if you can't be seen with me?"

He rubbed the back of his neck. He was sweating, and may have been a little drunk besides. "I never thought you'd come into Jimmy's, for God's sake," he muttered.

"Yeah, well, as master of the unexpected, I did. But your spangleprat friends tossed me out like a rotten melon, while you made love to your drink. I guess when the joint runs out of beef blood, you can always fill the bill with Bloody Marys."

Carlozo grew a little indignant, sort of like Jack grew a little beanstalk. To say he had a short fuse implied he had any kind of fuse at all. He ran off his mouth about the sterling character of every flyer in there, especially Jimmy, who Carlozo described like a benevolent country squire for all of them. He made it sound like it was my fault in the first place and I deserved to be tossed out of the Hi-Wire for presuming to barge into their tree house.

"Can we finish this later?" I finally said. "My leg's fallen asleep and I wanna put it to bed."

He paused and wiped a hand over his face. "Have you located my wife?"

"You know the answer to that, ya phony baloney. I followed one stinkin' lead on your wife and ended up with a star-back seat watching a poor sap test Newton's law. By the way, Newton is still right."

The flyer smoothed his mustache with his thumbnail. "I didn't know this man Bork," he said.

"That's nanty to me, Carlozo. I'm washing my hands of this."

"No, you cannot quit! No one quits on me!"

"Listen, my rep's bad enough as it is. Once word gets around Top Town that I was with Bork before he went south, even the lice will leave me alone. Now scram, and let me ruin my life my own way. Get somebody other than me."

"I."

"Darn right, 'aye'. What, you're a Scotsman now?"

"No, 'I'. 'I'."

"Yea or nay! Aye or nigh! What d'ye mean? Spit it oot, laddie!"

He closed his eyes and reined in that Gaelic temper. "Listen, Koko . . ."

"And another thing: You said I should bring your wife back so you can kill her. I shrugged it off. It sounded like so much elephant wash until Bork ended up dead."

Remembering what he said this morning brought the first hint of shame to Carlozo's face. "That was a mistake. I was angry, you can understand. A man's pride is worth fighting for."

"Is it worth killing for?"

"I had nothing to do with Bork!" he insisted. "And I . . . I will of course not kill my wife. I've never harmed her in my life. I just want her home, safe."

We were both startled when the door to the bar banged open and a couple of joeys staggered out, still shaky from guffaws. They didn't notice us, as they turned up the street in search of new yuks. When we were alone again, I said, "Get somebody else to do it. Get Jimmy Plummett—maybe he can find time between body waxes."

Carlozo was silent for a while. He looked a lot less imposing here in the street than he did in Daisy's stall this morning. Maybe he'd hired me because he had no more favors to call in with his regular gang. I had a little sympathy for him then, but not much. I was just about to head back into the bar when Carlozo fished a wad of cash out of his pocket. He peeled off five twenties, grabbed my hand and pressed the bills into it. "You cannot quit," he said firmly, "I will not let you. Find my wife. I know you are the man for the job."

I stared at my hand in amazement. A wad that big felt so un-usual, I half-believed it was someone else's arm coming out of my sleeve. Before I could come to my senses and respond, Carlozo was already walking away.

CHAPTER 7

Big Dog, Little Dog

Carlozo headed up Clown Alley toward Kelly, walking so fast that a few dogs started nipping at his heels. I pocketed the money he'd forced on me, sat down on a stoop and lit up a gasper. My situation now was a puzzle. If I'd really quit the job, was I now a freelancer with a big tip? Should I have thrown his money back at him, or was that simply a physical impossibility for me? Was I just being picky about who I'd let push me around, preferring the ones with ready cash? And how could I satisfy my own curiosity and find this Boots Carlozo without tipping anybody off to what I was doing? All it would take is brains, finesse, stealth and tenacity. Lucky for me, there wasn't one of them I couldn't spell.

I was getting up to leave when a large brown sedan pulled up to the curb. Out of the driver's side came a stocky, pug-nosed guy in a blue suit. As he walked around the car toward me, the passenger door opened. On top of the seat sat a peach basket, and on top of the peach basket sat a midget. He wore a tailored suit much nicer than his partner's, and an expression as cuddly as a keg of nails. He jumped off his perch and walked over like he had a lot of better things to do.

The first guy said, "We're looking for a guy named Koko."

"What would you do with him when you found him?"

The midget piped up, "This is him, Tom. Gotta be."

The big one looked at me expressionless and said, "I'm Detective Tom Kashaw, Spaulding Police. This is Detective Piscopink. We'd like to ask you a few questions."

"Seems fair," I said. "You want me to answer them, too?"

"Up to you. We can make this easy or we can make it hard."

"Is it multiple choice, or essay question?"

"Just answer them in full and you'll earn extra credit," said Kashaw.

"I forgot to bring a No. 2 pencil," I said, "and my brother ate my homework."

The midget came up under my nose and sneered, "Keep it up, pal, and you can stay after class for a couple days downtown."

The regular-size cop changed the metaphoric theme on us, and none too soon. "You know a Berndt Bork?"

"Excuse yourself," I said, "and go get a Bromo."

A blinding pain from my shins buckled me over and forced me back onto the stoop. "You think we got all day to do-si-do with you, clown?" asked the midget.

Kashaw said, "Listen, funnyboy: I'm talking about a guy named Bork, first name Berndt, age unknown, but not getting any older, on accounta he died a bizarre death. Although in this part of town, 'bizarre' is a relative term."

I patiently explained to him in minute detail, "I don't know nothin', I never did know nothin', and I don't plan on knowin' nothin' for the foreseeable future."

(Out of long habit, us kinkers never cooperate with cops. There's a couple dozen reasons for this, but the main one is that when a kinker gets tossed in the hoosegow for questioning or worse, it can stop a show dead in its tracks. No one, but no one, is expendable if a show's to make its next stand. Helping the local bulls can lead to a bankrupt show and a bunch of kinkers out of work in the middle of the season, at which point we begin to eat our young. We don't need cops anyway. We've got our own ways of dealing with trouble.)

Piscopink came up and said, "You might wanna start knowing something soon. We got a witness says she saw you going into Bork's yard just before he had his accident."

"Who you gonna believe, me or some crummy witness? I been here since lunchtime; go in and ask the goat. I don't go hanging out with daredevils anyway. Bad for your health."

Kashaw paused, then said, "You said you didn't know him. How'd you know he was a daredevil?"

"You guys are all wet," I snapped. "I been keepin' my nose clean."

"That's a full time job, obviously," said the midget.

"Maybe it explains the mess all over your coat," said the other cop.

"What?"

"There's stains all over it. You a sloppy eater?"

"When I need to be."

Piscopink looked closer. "A lot of this is monkey poo, which shouldn't be surprising. And creampies, typical. But these handprints. Looks like axle grease to me. You been busy in the garage—ha!—working on one of your teeny cars?"

"Yeah, well, I have to," I said. "What else am I gonna do? Leave it in the hands of a midget mechanic?"

Piscopink's little ears reddened. There's only two reasons midgets and clowns can't get along: midgets like him, and clowns like me. "Don't push your luck, Pagliacci," he said. "We're gonna crack this case open, and no one's gonna care how we do it, or who we have to bust up to get it done. One clown more or less won't matter to anybody."

"One last question, Koko," said Kashaw. "Did any of you circus people have anything against the mayor?"

"Mayor? What mayor?"

"The mayor of Spaulding, Eugene X. Brody."

"Never heard of the stiff. This place has a mayor? What's he do?"

"Whaddya mean, 'what's he do'? He runs the city."

"Really? When does he start?"

The cops left me with dismissive snorts and warnings to not leave town. But why in heaven's name would I want to? So far today Top Town had been such a lollapalooza.

Behind me someone cleared his throat. I turned around slowly and saw Happy Jingles in the doorway of the Peel, smiling and beckoning me with a crooked finger. Oh yeah. A real lollapalooza.

CHAPTER 8

Follow the Queen

Leaving aside the cash in hand (which would disappear altogether if I ran into any more creditors), the day had not been a big improvement on any in the recent past. I was just sober enough to witness the spectacle. And now I had a cop with a big chip on his weensy shoulder, ready to hang a permanent "Kick Me" sign on my back. I tell ya, nothing can larry up your life faster than a midget with a badge.

But as much as I disliked Carlozo, he was trusting me with this job. A rare position to find myself in, rare enough to not toss aside. In a lot of corners around Top Town, thanks to the backstage whisperers and old wives carrying tales, my name was already mud. If I didn't do something to clear my name from suspicion about Bork, it'd be mud with a twist of mud, and a double-mud chaser. The stink wouldn't go away on its own. Giving up now would bring too much pleasure to the gossips, the sneaks, and the tinpot bullies like Piscopink. Yeah, I'd done enough ducking and weaving. It was time to stop and take a pie.

I headed north toward Kelly, on my way to visit Flying Fleming. Mardo Street was a dukey run over to the east side, but maybe I could get there, find the skirt, wrap this up before dark, and go back to ignoring flyers and daredevils. God knows, there's only so much crap you can pack into one day.

As I walked, the whine of Piscopink's voice filled my head like a swarm of bees. There was something about that little copper that didn't bode well. He wasn't just a shakedown artist, or a backroom sadist, or a power-mad bully. He was all those things, plus a few more. My temples throbbed and my hands clenched as I imagined our next meeting. A bounce developed in my step worthy of Joe Louis. As I ran through violent though satisfying daydreams, I began to notice how sharp the hay and horse sweat in the Hippodrome smelled, and it brought back the memories of many a fine summer day on the road. The breeze shook the bare lightbulbs hanging along a wire like ripe pears ready to fall. I could smell the peppery tang of sausages cooking somewhere nearby and that tomb-like odor of ozone from an electrical generator clanking away on the corner. All around me, Top Town seemed louder, brighter, grittier, crazier than it had been in a long time. I guess it can help your mood immensely to have someone special you'd like to smother in a shoebox.

I walked down Kelly toward Fratellini Circle, the hub that connects a tangle of streets at the south end of Top Town. In the middle of the circle is a red granite tower three stories tall, dedicated to the memory of some forgotten hero from the War of 1812. This morbid, overwrought hitching post is in general only useful to acrobats, who like to practice tricks on it. Even then, I noticed two way up top, dangling their legs over the side and having a smoke at the foot of Admiral Whosis. The sun had set, and the flatties had begun to swarm into town again, and those two pongers up there had the perfect view to enjoy it all.

On the way to Mardo Street, I realized I hadn't eaten anything but biscuits and beer all day, so I stopped by a grease joint and bought a couple of corn dogs and a candy apple. I figured it would be good to have a healthy meal in me if I had to tangle with an Amazon, a copper or, as my luck would have it, any random stranger I might happen to pass.

Mardo is a short, narrow, unpaved path—basically a glorified shortcut. It was easy enough to find Fleming's place. Four large canvas banners walling off his lot proclaimed him the daringest devil of them all, painted with scenes hinting that a man is only truly in his element when he's falling from 5,000 feet. Unlike Bork, intent on practicing to perfect his act and take it on the road, it looked like Fleming was content to run his own show here a dozen times a night, charging the elmers two bits to watch. Fleming himself was there in front, selling tickets at a rickety podium.

He didn't look anything at all like the plucky, plunging youth depicted on his banners, swooping down past shocked para-troopers and envious eagles. A doughy fella about 50, with wild, receding hair that hadn't seen a comb today, he wore a suit jacket shiny at the elbows, a baggy undershirt and a red aviator's scarf. While his career of defying Death may have been successful in an ultimate sense, it had left him with some imposing scars on his head and neck. He had a vacant expression as he droned through his spiel and sold ducats to the crowd. I waited until the tip was gone before I went up.

"Business looks good," I said.

After a pause, he said, "Could always be better. Sorry, no Annie Oakleys."

"I didn't come to see you impersonate a lemming. I'm here on business."

Fleming squinted one eye and sized me up. "If it's anything but selling brushes, I ain't interested." Taking a silver flask from his coat pocket, he took a long swallow with nary a choke, sigh or whoop.

"And if I *were* selling brushes?"

"I'd tell you where to put one, and how hard to scrub."

"Hey, don't give me the runaround. That's my job. I'm looking for . . ."

"I know what you want. You came to see if I was shaking in my shoes. Well, nuts to you, and double nuts to your boss. You can tell him I got his message and he don't scare me."

"Message? He knows . . . ?"

"If your boss tries any rough stuff, he'll find I can still defend myself. Although, if he's sending around joeys to do his dirty work, maybe I got nothin' to worry about—he must be buried up to the axles." He laughed scornfully and lubricated his nerves again.

"You always get so juiced up before your act, Fleming?" I asked.

"Listen, zany, I been doing my act for more than 20 years, and a lot more besides. Swallowed swords, wrestled bears, even been buried alive. Hooch never hurts me. Doesn't even affect me."

"What's with the attitude, Fleming? You don't think my client has a legit beef with you?"

"Ooooh. 'Client.' Isn't that rich?" He chortled low and mean, like the Little Engine That Couldn't Care Less. "'Client' makes it all sound so legal, so official."

"He just wants what's his."

"Tell him to go to hell," snapped Fleming. "What happened was a long time ago. I didn't even know he was still around, but I'm ready for whatever he's got to dish out."

"Huh? What are you talking about?"

"I know what happened to Bork," Fleming sneered, "but I ain't running."

"You're nuttier than most daredevils I've met, and that's saying something. Just tell me where Boots is and I'll be on my way."

"Boots?" he asked. "Whaddya want with Boots? Boots ain't here."

"I don't believe you."

"Tough," he spat, getting uncomfortably close. Some of his scars, I was beginning to realize, might not have come from performances. "She ain't here, hasn't been for days. And if she *was* here, I wouldn't hand her over to a goon like you.

Now beat it. I got a show to do, and I don't want to see you around when I'm done." He took his reel of tickets and his cashbox and stepped behind his banners.

Despite his anger and the flecks of spit hanging from my eye-brows, I wanted more dope from Fleming after he did his belly-flop, so I snuck through the entrance quickly behind him and scooted left instead of right. About 15 people were scattered around three rickety sets of bleachers, with faces half-excited, half-solemn and worldly wise. The flatties of Spaulding think they've been around and seen it all, but the fact that they're still coming down and paying their money to be thrilled by someone else's recklessness tells you the whole story. Nobody noticed me except a big, red-headed young gink in dungarees and a checkered shirt. He followed me with bright eyes as I snuck beneath the stands.

The bleachers faced a platform raised three feet off the ground. In the middle sat an old washtub painted yellow with blue bands, while looming above it, festooned with faded cloth pennants, was the diving platform, about 40 feet up and tethered by four guy wires staked out in the corners of the lot. Towards the back of the lot was a small shack with dirty windows and a roof drooping over the front porch. About three minutes later, from inside the shack we heard a snare drum roll, followed by a cymbal crash. Fleming emerged through the front door, wearing blue bathing trunks and an undershirt sewn with blue piping and sequins. He wore canvas slippers on his feet, his bright red scarf still around his neck. He looked surprisingly focused and sober. He'd even combed his hair.

Lit by a pair of dinky spotlights nailed to the platform, Flying Fleming stepped up and addressed the audience: "Ladies and gentlemen, thank you for your applause, and welcome. Tonight, you will witness a feat so daring, so perilous, so absolutely amazing, that you will ponder anew the extent of human bravery and endurance."

Well, judging from the noise, the crickets thereabouts were impressed.

"Tonight, you'll witness as I laugh off danger and shrug at serious injury. You'll watch as I climb to that tiny perch, 87 feet above the ground, and dive headfirst into this shallow tub of water. Can it be done? Can any man survive such a plunge? I invite you all, ladies and gentlemen, to watch and marvel. A plunge from 87 feet in the air, into this shallow basin. I would ask the men in the audience to please hold onto their sweethearts, lest the excitement prove too much for their delicate nature. Behold, as I spit in the face of Death himself, for your entertainment!"

After a quick style, Fleming turned to the tub and inspected the depth of the water with his arm for some extra show. Apparently satisfied, he began climbing the skinny, swaying rope ladder up to his little perch. The elmers were watching with interest, but not with the open-mouthed awe that Fleming wanted to evoke. Once they saw Fleming's act, they'd probably shuffle on to the next attraction and stare again like hounds in August sunshine. My guess was it was getting harder and harder to impress people these days.

From where I was standing, nothing about the lot looked suspicious. But what the hell was I looking for, a picture of Carlozo scratched with devil horns and a goatee? As Fleming climbed, I snuck around under the stands, trying to get closer to his shack. There was probably no way to get in there and out while he did his act, but it seemed more productive than standing behind the bleachers staring at people's cabooses.

By the time Fleming was at the top, I was about 15 feet from his front door. I went no further, because he'd be able to see me dart in now and was due back on earth any second. Streams of pennants were tied from the top of his ladder to poles down on the ground, and a weather-beaten American flag hung beneath his platform. He stepped onto the tiny perch, threw his scarf over his shoulder, and looked down. "Ladies and gentlemen, please," he boomed after he caught his breath, "to perform this dangerous dive, I will need complete silence." Long, dramatic pause. "One . . ."

Before he could get to "two", a brittle crack was heard and a small piece of wood shot out from under the perch, trailing brightly in the lights like an ember. The figure of the high diver, which had been so ramrod straight, now crouched and shimmied as he tried to regain his balance. With another, louder crack, the perch fell away. Without a sound from either Fleming or his audience, he fell to earth, arms and legs waving, red scarf trailing behind handsomely. The diver smacked into the side of the tub with a thud, sending the water splashing high in the air and the dented tub skittering off like an empty can. From other parts of Top Town, faint sounds and music could be heard, but here, even the crickets were stunned.

At least he hit his target, which was more than you could say for Bork.

I rushed up to Fleming, with two other gees from the crowd. Glistening in the lights, his wet, motionless body was tangled up like last year's scarecrow. I reached down to untangle him a bit and lay him on his back. Somebody else felt his neck, then pulled his eyelids closed.

Silence still gripped the crowd, so everyone jumped—someone even shrieked—when the door of the shack slammed shut loudly. As if materializing out of thin air by the magic of the crash, a blond woman in khaki slacks was now racing for the exit. She'd likely been watching the whole grisly scene from the shack. When the crowd saw her, it was like she'd reminded them they weren't glued to their seats. They all took off running for the street too, not wanting to hang around for the cops. I followed, because the blond woman had to be Boots Carlozo.

The tangle of people running for the exit didn't slow me down much, but out on Mardo Street the evening's foot traffic did. To my left a few blocks was the waterfront, to my right was Slivers Street and the route back to the lights and hullabaloo of Griebling. Boots could've either run for cover or try and hide in plain sight among the flatties strolling along.

I didn't like my chances down by the docks, where even the rats traveled in pairs for safety, so I turned right and headed up into the crowd.

I trotted along, looking sideways into alleys and around corners for a glimpse of that striking blond hair. All I snagged were a couple of elmers who thought it was big laughs to run behind me and mimic my unique style of running. At first, the amateur clowning and mocking "hyuk-yuk-yuks" didn't bother me, but as more time dribbled away without a trace of Boots, these guys began raising my usually flaccid hackles. I told them to buzz off, but they just grinned in my face, like we were all partners in the joke.

"Herman, please," said a young woman looking on from a distance. "Leave him alone. I'm scared of clowns. You *know* I'm scared of clowns."

One of my pursuers (Herman, I'm guessing) waved her off with a Bronx cheer. Again she pleaded with him, and he ignored her. So I kept trotting and the two elmers followed behind again, to the crowd's amusement. I sped up the sidewalk, and they sped up the sidewalk. I zigged, and they zagged. Coming up on the left was a fortune teller's shop with a closed Dutch door. I scooted over and, still running, hammered on the door as hard as I could. My pursuers did the same thing. Cutting a quick figure eight, I rapped on the door again. Likewise, my pals. Relying on timing and the short temper of a gypsy trying to pry money from a gullible mark, I circled round a third time. Just as I raised my hand again, the angry mitt reader opened the top half of the door out. With a flea's hiccup to spare, I ducked and ran under. Lacking the proper training and reflexes, my innocent playmates barreled full speed into the door, as the gypsy screamed in surprise.

"Shoulda listened to her, Herman," I said over my shoulder.

How badly they were hurt, I got no idea, but the door sounded like it held up pretty well. I didn't stick around for a curtain call, but gave up on Boots and tried to get back to Fleming's place before the cops sauntered over.

CHAPTER 9

Marked Cards

At Fleming's lot, the lights were still on and the pennants were flying, but the place showed as much life as a sandbag. I pulled aside the big canvas that blocked the entrance and walked inside. Up on the platform lay Fleming, looking like he was grabbing 40 winks. I tried to be careful and not leave tracks in the wet dust with my 42s. A crowd had seen me there, and had seen me run out with them. I didn't need a lot of physical evidence to back up their accounts of the accident.

When Fleming fell, I have to admit, I had to stop myself from running out and doing some shtick to get the crowd laughing. Don't peg me as some sort of ghoulish scene-stealer. It's just something clowns have done for years. Whenever another performer gets hurt or an act goes wrong, clowns are supposed to run out and distract people while the injured are helped off. The show must go on, after all, so clowns are the first ones out there to use their magic to chase away thoughts of pain and death. By the way, if you're ever in the audience and hear the band play the old Sousa tune "Stars and Stripes Forever," look around and get ready to get the hell out. That song's a signal to us kinkers that there's some kind of emergency. Of course, sometimes things fall apart so fast, the band doesn't even get a chance to play it.

I might get five uninterrupted minutes to inspect Fleming's shack, so I went to work snooping around. The porch was just some planks laid on the ground and an overhang roof held up by shaky two-by-fours. There was no screen door, so I pulled open the flimsy front door and tiptoed in. Fleming's snare drum and cymbal stood just inside, but I somehow avoided knocking them over; I'll have to write that one in my diary someday, as soon as I start keeping one. A small oil lamp on a table displayed a room that was spartan and tattered. The brown wood stove against the wall was still warm, though the grease of a neglected pan of meat had congealed on top. A kiester beside it held a pile of flashy clothes. I rummaged through there but found nanty. Ditto behind the curtain that marked off where the army cots were placed for a sleeping room.

Fleming had acted like such a lush, I was curious how orderly he kept his place. While things weren't particularly tidy in here, it didn't look like Fleming had turned into a boozy bum. My guess was he'd kept his equipment in adequate shape, too. A daredevil who didn't look after his equipment, after all, was basically a suicide on the installment plan, and Fleming had impressed me as a fighter, not a quitter. Without even looking at it, I knew his platform had been gaffed. Which made this a murder. Which made me a witness to murder twice over today. Which made the corn dogs in my stomach do a flip.

The rickety table was cluttered with racing forms and empty bottles. I poked around on it, looking for some decent epitaph for this gink. Amid all the garbage was something odd: A single red playing card. I flipped it over and found a queen of hearts, on which was written in big black letters: "Pierre 1928." There were no other cards on the table, no deck it was missing from. Was this some kind of souvenir? A card from an admirer? A handout for a new restaurant in town?

I slipped the playing card into my pocket and gave the place one more look-see. On the walls were hung a few girly pictures and some yellowed postcards, but by the front door was a poster shouting so loud I could barely hear myself think. Ripped and stained though it was, the crimson and gold colors were as vivid as the Sunday funnies. The poster advertised an old Cannon & Crowley show and had a couple of ferocious, pouncing tigers printed above an ornate frame listing the attractions. It mentioned Thursday, July 11, but no year. Among the marvels it promised the audience were, "The Three Aerial Aces, Miraculous, Stupendous, Astounding."

Berndt Bork.

"Flying" Fleming.

Reynaldo Carlozo.

Three aces. A triumvirate of short-tempered talent. So, Carlozo had been playing dumb about these kinkers. Big mistake. It's always a bad idea to play dumb with a clown. You'll never win.

I ripped the poster off the wall, folded it into my coat pocket and left the shack. Fleming's body still lay in the spotlight, but I couldn't bring myself to look at it again. I went to the back of the lot to look for a way out and escaped through a gap in the fence. For the next couple hours, I prowled the streets looking for Boots Carlozo, like a wily jungle cat in floppy shoes. To keep overexcited fans from following me again, I stuck to the shadows and doorways. Thanks to this afternoon's accident, a few extra flatfoots were out, not knowing what to be watching for. But from the freak shows to the cooch shows, and every type of act or attraction in between, there was no sign of Boots anywhere.

I asked myself, what did it really mean that those three had been on a show together? This could have been a feud among flyers. Maybe something was said or done that got their leotards in a bunch, so that years later . . . they start killing each other? Seemed a little hysterical, but these guys weren't exactly Presbyterian ministers. Fleming was plenty burned up to know I was working for Carlozo, like I was hired muscle or something. Bork and Carlozo both said they didn't know each other, so either the poster was bogus or they were.

Another thing they shared, to put it ungallantly, was Boots. Maybe she'd gone round the bend and turned bloodthirsty, and Carlozo wanted her back for her own safety. But Bork and Fleming were both sabotaged, not sliced open in their sleep. They were killed efficiently, spectacularly—but not in the heat of passion. Besides, while Bingo mentioned something about a black widow, no one had described Boots as loony-bin material yet. In her exit from Fleming's, she looked like a rabbit flushed from her hole. Maybe she was the target and the killer just had incredibly lousy timing.

A third possibility—one that got my heart racing—was that somebody wanted to frame *me* for all this mess. The cops sure found me awful fast after Bork bought the farm. Maybe that's why Carlozo snubbed me but insisted I keep after his wife, so he'd know exactly where to find me. OK, maybe this was a little paranoid, but just because you're paranoid doesn't mean someone isn't out to get you.

All these possibilities just didn't add up. I needed more dope, and without Boots, the only other source was her husband. I was pretty sure where I could find him, but by this time of night, Jimmy's Hi-Wire would be filled to the frames with fried funambulists. If I stuck my head in there again, they might not give it back. But I went up near there anyway and half a block away spied a kid hanging out on the corner.

"Hey there, little feller," I said, nice and friendly. "Your old buddy Rex needs some help here. If you take a message into that tavern there and give it to a man inside, why—hooo-hooo-hooo!—I'd just be ever so grateful!"

The bip stared at me without emotion.

"Would you do it for a balloon animal and a nice lollipop?" I asked sweetly.

My little pal perked up and smiled, "I'd do it for two bucks and a cigarette."

Used to be, I could spot the locals. My little extortionist waited patiently while I took a grease pencil and wrote on the poster from Fleming's shack. I drew a line through the names of the two dead flyers, with a small skull and crossbones and a question mark, in case Carlozo was too plastered to appreciate subtlety. I then wrote, "Meet me?" and handed the folded poster to the kid. After describing Carlozo to him, I said, "Now, you got to promise me to put this right in his hand. Cross your heart and hope to die."

Again, like talking to a waxwork dummy.

"OK, just promise me to get it in his hand before you drink up this cash."

The kid smiled. "You got it, bigshoe."

After a few minutes, the kid came out, handed me the poster and headed back inside the bar. On the poster was written, "10 AM, Landon & Grimaldi."

It was past 9 o'clock now. Today had been exhausting, and had started way too early. I couldn't think straight anymore. Bingo had offered me his hammock for a kip, so I began to walk the couple of blocks to his wagon. Above the flashing lights and the neon rainbow of the street, the warm night was black and starless, with a refreshing breeze coming from the harbor. The tinny music from the band organs and the voices of the spielers began to fade as I dragged my tired body to Bingo's, and I thought of how unfair it was that such a beautiful evening could wind up having a tack on every seat.

CHAPTER 10

Read 'Em and Weep

The next morning opened bright and still, the kind of morning, if memory deceives, that always occurred on the road. A cool sweet morning, shiny as a new nickel, a nickel you could never lose, spend or be cheated out of. I pulled myself out of the hammock and stretched what I had left to stretch with. Bingo was nowhere to be seen around his wagon; he must've found a jill last night who needed those things only a clown can give.

With a few simoleons in my pocket, I decided to skip my usual breakfast of stolen apples and filched milk and dine with the other fine citizens of Top Town at the Pie Car. I headed in the direction of Fox Street, stepping carefully to avoid the empty bottles, popcorn boxes, finked prizes and other leftovers from the night before. I felt like checking out yesterday's baseball scores, so I sauntered over to the sidewalk shack of Hobie Hoobler, the old blind newsie, to get a copy of the daily fishwrap. Because old habits die hard, I snuck up to the shack and tried to eyeball the paper from a distance.

"Should I move the stand a little closer?" asked Hobie from behind his smoked glasses. "I'd hate for you to strain your eyes, Rex."

"Er, g'morning, Hobie."

He cracked a little smile, his amber stub of a cigarette still pinched between thin lips. "Some awful news yesterday, ah?"

I picked up the front page of the paper and remembered that two kinkers fell to their deaths yesterday under mysterious circumstances just after I'd had words with them. Maybe today wouldn't be as sunny and fancy-free as I'd thought.

Splashed over three columns, the *Spaulding Oracle* related how the car of Mayor Eugene X. Brody had been struck by a "circus performer traveling through the air at a high rate of speed." They even printed a diagram of the events, with heavy dotted lines and black arrows arching over the map like some Rube Goldberg cartoon. Bork's final landing spot was marked with a Maltese cross. The picture of Mayor Brody made him look shifty, bug-eyed and guilty. Nothing new there; that was the way he always looked. They printed two pictures of Berndt Bork: one a publicity still from at least ten years ago, the other pic of his crumbled body in the shiny suit lying in the street. The mayor's car was never pictured, my guess being that he rabbitted out of there after the accident.

"Did ya know this guy, Bork?"

"No, why would I?" I said, too quickly.

"Just wonderin'. You appreciate, I'm a nosy newsie."

In a sidebar editorial, the paper was calling for the mayor's head. Scandalous. Corrupt. Debauched. Repugnant. And that just described his suit.

"Hey, read to me what the paper says about Brody. It cracks me up."

I cleared my throat and read, "'The moral infection of this administration on Spaulding cannot be allowed to continue. Eugene X. Brody has brought shame and dishonor to this city. What was he doing in that disreputable slum in the middle of the day? His answer is, "Researching ways to improve the lives of the citizens of Top Town." If he thinks anyone believes this, he's as big an ignoramus as he is a

62

thief.' Reading between the lines, I'd say the *Oracle* doesn't care for the guy."

"Well, with a publisher like Pierpont, I'm not surprised. He still thinks Lincoln was a commie for freeing the slaves."

"How do you suppose Brody plans to 'improve' our lives down here in the slum?"

"Don't make me laugh," said Hobie. "Nothing's going to clean up Top Town very soon, especially a politician who's had a taste of freak show lovin'. He ain't the first 'respectable' person to find himself caught on Nock Street, and he won't be the last."

"Yep, they never stop. Who can blame them? There's more than one reason they call Betty Blansky 'the Ostrich Girl'."

A voice behind us said, "I concur, Mr. Hoobler, I concur." I turned around to see T.C. Montgomery over my shoulder, again looking as dapper as a rookie train conductor. "Brody won't clean up Top Town, but not because he's ineffectual."

"I hadn't heard that," I said. "So he's a little swishy. What's that got to do . . ."

"No, my fine clown," he corrected with a chuckle. "Ineffectual: bad at his job. He won't clean up Top Town because no one will clean it up. Top Town exists for many reasons, one of which is, it gives politicians a chance to bloviate."

"But wait, you said Brody *wasn't* a nancy-boy."

Montgomery looked at me blankly for a beat, then two, then three. "You've cleaned yourself up since yesterday, Mr. Koko. Quite an improvement. A change in your fortunes?"

"Yeah, bunches of changes."

Hobie coughed and plucked his cigarette from his lip. "So, Mr. Montgomery, you got a puzzler for me today?"

The frail financier said, "Yes, Mr. Hoobler, let me think. Ah, here's one:

'He who makes it, tells not;

He who uses it, knows not;

He who has it, wants it not.

What is it?'"

Hobie scratched his chin, flummoxed by this riddle. When an answer struck me, I raised my hand and pleaded, "Oooh, I know, I know, pick me! Pick me!"

Montgomery shook his head. This game was for Hobie only. The blind man grimaced with concentration, but eventually gave up.

"The answer, of course," said Montgomery like an old professor, "is counterfeit money. Ha ha. That was your answer, was it not, Mr. Koko?"

I lied and said sure it was. Besides, who'd ever heard of a laxative cream pie?

As Montgomery picked up a paper and limped away without paying, I asked Hobie what just happened. He was pretty sore to admit it, but said every morning Montgomery came around, he pitched Hobie a puzzler. If he solved it, Hobie would win a dollar; if not, he gave up a free paper. In the two years this had been going on, Hobie had been a winner exactly zero times.

"Hobie, I'm surprised at you. In the words of the immortal Barnum . . ."

"I know, I know," he said testily, "'There's a sucker born every minute.'"

"'And two to take him.'" Hobie grew sullen after that, so I paid for my paper and left.

If you want to eat something other than popcorn and cotton candy around here, about the only place to get it is the Pie Car. There's no sign to mark it, but if the orange and blue "Hotel" flag is up, they're still serving. Housed in an old converted train car, the joint was started by Paco and Pedro Morales, a couple of Mexican brothers with an aerial act. One day they had a falling out (not literally, thank god), and now Pedro slung the hash while his wife Sarasota Rosie slung the bull with the customers up front. They were a couple of good eggs; Rosie in particular always treated me kind.

I slid into a booth, although not one by the front windows. I was a little on edge, expecting to be met soon by a police squadron, 14 creditors, nine insulted acquaintances, and three or four women with babes in arms and angry looks on their faces. Even the murmur of the people gobbling their eggs seemed to be all about me. It takes a lot of ego to be this paranoid, believe me. I jumped when Rosie snuck up behind me and slapped a menu down.

"Hello, stranger," she said with a smile. "To what do we owe the pleasure?"

"Well, I'm hungry," I said, "and I've got money. How's that for a start?"

"Sounds OK. You haven't been around for a while. I was beginning to think you didn't like Pedro's cooking, because I *know* you still like my company."

"All I wanna know is, with the war winding down, what's Pedro going to do when the Army stops buying his biscuits?"

Rosie looked at me puzzled. "The Army has their own bakers."

"Yeah, but their biscuits can't pierce tank armor like Pedro's."

Rosie laughed again, her white teeth looking extra bright against the lustrous dark hair of her beard. "I'll have to tell him that one."

"Tell him *after* he cooks my food, okay?"

Rosie took my order and brought me a cup of coffee. I was pouring sugar into a spoon when someone leaped into the booth across from me and jostled the table, spraying sugar all over. I looked up, about to sputter something witty yet forceful, and saw my dining companion was fugitive-of-the-hour Boots Carlozo. Her blond hair was held back with a red scarf, revealing a long, solid, well-built face. She wore no makeup but had a healthy glow and a directness that made her instantly attractive. Under vanilla-custard eyebrows, her eyes were blue and clear, but anchored by bags big enough for a trip to Argentina. This was the only part of her that hinted at trouble, aside from her clenched fists and bared teeth.

"What do you want from me?" she demanded. "Why do you keep following me?"

"Hey now, I don't 'keep' following you. I've barely been able to find you. You gave me the slip pretty well in the crowd last night."

"Cut the baloney. You're following me. Just because you can't do it without wrecking people's lives is beside the point."

"Listen, I'm not trying to wreck anyone's life. I'm busy enough wrecking my own. And it's a damn shame that Bork and Fleming died, but I had nothing to do with it."

"Don't sell yourself short," she scoffed.

"What do you mean?"

"You're Rex Koko, right?"

Suddenly her bluntness wasn't quite so appealing. "You know the answer to that, I guess," I muttered.

"Yeah, so maybe I got reason to be concerned."

"Ah, nothing starts the day off right like an insult from a pretty woman. I'm following you because your husband wants you back home. He's hired me to be the Pied Piper."

"Hired you? Like a private dick or something?" Her voice con-tained an unflattering amount of disbelief.

"Yeah, he did. Nothin' to drop your jaw about. I've done a lot of this work before."

"And I'm supposed to find that comforting?"

"You're not dealing with an amateur, that's all."

"Thank heaven for that," she said with a wave of her hand. "Who knows what kind of mess an amateur might've made of it? Oooh, my head. What's the word for when the shame of a situation is only overmatched by its indignity?"

"You're asking the wrong guy, toots." I began tapping more sugar into my spoon. "Anyway, after I have my breakfast, which you are welcome to join me in, I suggest we visit your husband so we can work this all out."

"Oh yes, let's do," she said sarcastically. "It sounds fabulous. Why should we let a few murders get in the way of a happy reunion? Do you and Reynaldo have your knives all ready, or should we make a date for noon-ish? And what about your cowboy pal?"

"Don't start tossing accusations around, lady. I told you, I had nothing to do with Bork and Fleming."

"And what makes you think I did?"

"Because you got a such rep around town that . . ." I stopped, and she raised her eyebrows at me to underscore the point.

"Welcome to the club, clown."

She sat back and smoothed out the front of her red bolero jacket, letting me stew a bit. So in addition to her aerial skills, this Boots Carlozo was quite a knife thrower. As I pulled the knife out from between my eyes, I realized she was right. I'd let the gossip lead me along because it was a juicy story, not because it was getting me anywhere.

"OK, let's back up a bit. Answer me a few questions and maybe I'll leave you alone. Who's this cowboy you're talking about?"

"Some big red-headed clod. Every time I turn around, he's somewhere nearby."

"Has he ever said anything to you?"

"No. Whenever I call him out, he tries to disappear."

Thinking back to Fleming's audience, I asked, "Does he wear dungarees and a checked shirt?"

"You know him?"

"I think I know his brothers. Now listen, you and Carlozo, you're really married, right? None of this 'Billboard wedding' kind of stuff?"

Boots gritted her teeth and gave me a good slap across the chops. I was so surprised, my spoonful of sugar went sailing across the diner and landed in someone's eggs. From the other side of the room, someone shouted, "Hey clown, no food fights!"

"Looks like I struck a nerve," I said, rubbing my jaw, "while you might've severed a couple."

"My marriage is none of your business," she said.

"Lady, you got *no* idea how I wish that were true, but since your husband dragged me into this mess and kinkers started heading south like Canadian geese, it is my business, and I have to start asking some obvious questions."

She sighed and crossed her arms. "Like what?"

"Like, can I borrow your spoon? And the sugar?"

She closed her eyes and held them shut, as if I'd somehow disappear when she opened them. When that didn't work, she began to spill a little more. "I've been married to Reynaldo—in a church, with a priest—for nine years. For the most part it's been OK. He was at the top of his game back then, really swept me off my feet. I suppose a part of me still loves him now, despite his bullying and his vanity."

"He's well groomed," I offered. "And fit."

She snorted. "Yeah, 'fit.' Fit as a man half his age, he'll never tire of telling you. Only that's not the whole picture. Let's just say, he can't make me fly like he used to."

"Problems with his grip?" I pondered. "Maybe a little extra rosin . . ."

"Problems with his rigging. Yeah, how about that? You can im-agine what that did to his ego. He had his heart set on starting a dynasty—you know, sons and daughters to train and carry on his legacy." She took a drink of water from my glass and paused. Her voice lost some of its sauce. "It got to where I couldn't stand to watch it happening, to see his confidence dry up and rage take its place. When our farm was failing and my father started to act like this, I ran away and joined the circus. Now that I've been in the circus, where else can I run? I told Reynaldo it was no big deal, but every little white lie I told him only made him angrier. My god, what is it about you men and your crotches? Hey you, both hands on the table!"

"Sorry, just checking inventory."

We were interrupted by Rosie bringing over my pork chop and fried tomato breakfast. Making a queasy face, Boots declined my offer to get something for herself. Rosie gave me a look and retreated discretely. She was trying to add up what was going on at this table, but the advanced calculus stumped her.

"So the King of the Air couldn't get off the ground? There are worse things in life."

"What's a clown know about it?" she asked bitterly. "You guys never have those problems. You can satisfy any girl one way or another, from what I've heard. You know, 'the grin you can't wipe off'?"

"Stereotypes . . ."

"Whatever the case," she went on, "don't give me advice on marriage. You don't know me well enough."

"Sure, whatever you say. But even a dope like me can spot a few things. You might be worried about your husband, but you're worried about yourself, too. Like, 'if he can't fly, what does that say about me? Maybe I'm heading over the hill.' You're a jill who needs the spotlight, I can tell . . ."

"Hold on," she interrupted, "not everybody needs . . ."

"And," I continued, "and if Carlozo couldn't perform, there were other flyers around town who could fill out the act. And please don't slap me again; I'm trying to eat my breakfast while it's hot, with teeth if possible."

Boots lowered her arm, but still glared at me. After a silence, she said quietly, "You don't know what you're talking about."

"Doesn't mean I'm wrong," I said. "Now, tell me about Bork and Fleming."

Boots began to rub her temples tiredly. "Not much to tell. They gave me a place to stay."

"Had you known them a while?"

"Fleming, yes. Not Bork. We were introduced a couple weeks ago."

"Introduced?"

"By Jimmy Plummett, at his club. Bork was nice at first. Sent me little notes, as if he were courting me. Then, when I finally got fed up with Reynaldo and left, I show up at Bork's place, and he's changed. No fire at all. He let me stay, but he seemed more surprised than interested."

"Then you left to go to Fleming's."

"I thought I'd be safe there, until Reynaldo cooled off. Give us both some time." She stopped and bit her lip. "They didn't deserve to die like that. They were both getting their acts together, ready to start earning money. They'd each lost a lot at poker lately."

"Did you know that Bork and Fleming shared the bill with your husband with the Cannon & Crowley show a few years back?"

Boots shook her head. "Not until I saw that poster at Barney's. Reynaldo never mentioned it."

"Barney? Who the hell's Barney?"

"Fleming, you dope. Do you think his parents named him Flying?"

"I've heard worse," I said. "Did Fleming ever mention a guy named Pierre?"

"No. Hey, do you think that some gamblers might have done it, like the guys were in debt or something?"

"Probably not," I said. "A corpse is pretty crummy at paying off debts. Maybe there's something else going on, but my gut tells me your husband had a hand in it. You think Reynaldo could've gaffed the rigging?"

"Reynaldo?" she asked. "He's capable of anything."

"You don't say," I said, as a chill spread through my BVDs.

"Sure," she said, looking at me with those cool, blue eyes. "He hired you, didn't he?"

CHAPTER 11

Calling the Bluff

Boots lit out of the diner without another word. I could've grabbed her, I suppose, and marched her over to her hubby and be done with all of this. But I chose to sit back for a couple of reasons. First, if I'd tried to grab that wildcat, I could kiss my jaw goodbye. Second, I was pretty certain bringing her back wouldn't solve anything, and might make matters worse. Something else was going on here, and until I knew the kay fabe, it would be better to let things play out. This might've put her in danger, but I thought she could look after herself. She wasn't entirely clean in my book, either, which might mean others were in danger. Her husband might have been a danger to others and in danger himself. Me? Well, I ate danger for breakfast, although everyone who ate at the Pie Car could claim that.

As I got up from the booth and went to the counter to pay, every eye in the place turned to watch me. A bigger ham would've done a little dance for his exit, but I ignored the urge. I paid Rosie and took a toothpick from the jar. The silence of the room as I left was even more unnerving than the stares.

Outside on the steps, I tried to collect myself. Rested and gassed up, it was time to confront Carlozo with what I knew about his partners on the Cannon & Crowley show. If he was setting me up to be the patsy for the murders, I expect at least the common courtesy of telling me to my face. When I stepped to the sidewalk, I saw someone spying on me from across the street: the big, red-headed gink who'd been watching me at Fleming's lot.

I ran and shouted at him, but he slipped around the corner and disappeared. I dashed up Grimaldi, with no luck. About one block away, I saw a clutch of 15 people moving slowly like a herd of cattle in my direction. Leading the way were cops, both in uniform and plainclothes. In the middle of the pack was a nervous-looking man with a pale, flabby face, dirty blond hair, and bugged-out eyes that looked like they'd plead for mercy even when he was asleep. I recognized him from the papers: this morning's headline honey, Mayor Eugene X. Brody, followed by a group of bureaucrats, reporters and photographers.

The odd sight slowed me in my tracks until it was too late to get out of the way. The cops glared at me, resisting their instincts to bat me around with their batons. With the reporters and photogs around, I guess it was time to play nice in Top Town. I turned and tried to slip off into the shadows, when I heard a high, lilting voice say, "There, gentlemen, a fella from the neighborhood. Let's have a chat and a picture with him."

Two sets of hands grabbed me and roughly turned me around to face Mayor Brody. He was about my height and age, but his face was anxious and haggard, either from the guilt of his Catholic background or the strain of surviving Spaulding politics. A radiant sunburst that began in his nose and spread through the center of his face betrayed a fondness for the bottle. From the look of it, the papers had it right about Brody: a pliable princeling set up in the mayor's office by political bosses, as confident as a lion tamer wearing a porterhouse necktie. "G'mornin', how are ya?" he said, shaking my hand.

"Just ducky," I said, as dully as I could.

"Ha ha, I love a clown. Doesn't everybody love a clown?" Brody tried to get the reporters to chime in like a bunch of school kids, but these guys were saving their enthusiasm for something more exciting, like gutting Brody for these lame theatrics in tomorrow's papers. "When the world makes you weary, you can count on a clown for a good laugh, eh? Can you do a trick for us, son?"

"I can make $5 disappear," I said, putting my hand out.

This got a chuckle from everyone there. Brody said, "Oh, I've used that trick a few times meself, haha."

"I bet you have," I muttered.

"What's your name, son?" I told him and the reporters wrote it down. "I'm Gene Brody, mayor of this city, and I'd like to thank you for the opportunity to come down and meet some of Top Town's finest citizens like yourself."

"They're your sidewalks," I shrugged. "If you ain't gonna fix 'em, I suppose you can schmooze anyone you want on 'em."

A skinny flunky with pomaded hair urged the mayor to move on with his tour, but Brody said, "Nonsense, I find Mr. Kokomo here a delight to talk to. How about a picture, boys? Nothing captures all the positive things about Top Town like a funny clown, eh?" He reached his arm around my shoulder and began to exercise his gums: "I think clowns, and circus people of all stripes, have lessons to teach us, that what's past is firmly behind, and we should focus on what's up front, uniting and coupling with vigor and passion, to find the positions everyone can enjoy. That's why I've been coming here regularly . . . to get a leg up, or two or three, and thereby . . . fresh advances, bold moves . . . ripe as summer melons . . . in Spaulding as in ancient Rome . . . four or five at a time, until we all collapse, spent but satisfied with our efforts . . ."

His voice faded into the background like a sweet mist, and his arm felt so cozy and warm that I nodded off. I've learned over the years that, when the bluster gets too thick, especially from a politician, I just fall asleep on my feet like an old horse. I dreamed I was chasing butterflies in a field with Hedy Lamarr, who was sloppily enjoying a submarine sandwich, when I was startled awake by the flash of the camera bulbs.

"WHO? WHAT? Am I on?" I sputtered, to the great amusement of most of the crowd. Brody laughed so hard he started choking, which attracted more flashbulbs. I pounded him on the back, but his staff stepped in and forced me off. By the time Brody and his pack had moved on for more "fact-finding" with the good people of Top Town, I had the feeling the stories in the papers weren't going to be the sweet vindication he'd been planning. The best he could hope for was they might misspell his name.

All this nonsense almost made me late for my meeting with Carlozo. Whatever his mood might be this morning, I'd have to be ready for surprises if I wanted to survive until lunch. As I hustled over to Landon Street, I ran over a couple of opening lines in my head:

"You know how, last time we talked, there was only one dead body around? Funny thing . . ."

"So, problems with the ol' king pole, huh, Carlozo? My Uncle Oswald had the same thing . . ."

"So, today over breakfast your wife tells me . . ."

Nothing seemed to be that perfect ice-breaker I was looking for.

Not that it mattered any, because when I got to the corner, no one was waiting for me. Thanks to the mayor's parade, my mustachioed flyer might've flown off already. I stood around for about a minute until a harsh voice from behind me said, "Hey, clown, over here."

I looked at the ramshackle blacksmith shop where the voice came from. With no smoke coming out of the forge's chimney, the place looked abandoned. A wooden awning ran the length of the building front, casting a thick shadow in the bright morning sunshine. "Yeah, come over here." It wasn't Carlozo's voice, nor was it his style to sneak around like this.

"All right," I said, feeling edgy, "I'm always up for a talking horse gag. Who's good in the fifth race today, Sparkplug?" I approached the grimy shop slowly. Someone was standing in the shadows inside, but I couldn't tell who it was. By the time my eyes had adjusted to the dark, it was too late. Someone else hiding in the corner shoved me inside, and I stumbled into the grip of the first guy. It was Missouri Redd, his breath smelling like the bottom of a river.

"Boy, lamebrain," he laughed, "you sure fell for that one."

"Not as much as I'm falling for you, big boy."

He snarled at me, holding tight, "I'm here to give ya one warning, clown."

"Stay away from pumpkin-headed clodhoppers? But how can we deny the urgings of the heart?"

"Always with the smart mouth," he said. "Ya jes' think every-thing's a big joke, don't cha?"

"No, my Ozark sweetheart," I said, "I *know* everything's a big joke." He had my arms pinned but not my head, so I aimed my conk at the bridge of his nose and took a dive. My aim was perfect. The roustie howled and brought one hand to his face. I broke his grip, fell and rolled backwards, hoping to take out the guy behind me at the legs. I could only manage to throw him off balance. I pulled myself up on a hay bale and squared off with him. Now they were both where I could see them, but I was pinned in a corner.

"So, you another Redd Brother?" I asked, putting up my dukes.

"A-yuh."

"Which one are you? Wisconsin Redd? New Jersey Redd? Wait, I got it—Rhode Island Redd!"

"Nep," he said, trying a roundhouse punch I easily ducked.

"Don't tell me the family's gone international? That's downright frightening."

"Would be," he said, "ain't the case." He swung again and I dodged again.

"Hold on. How much would you tip a waitress on a tab of $2.15?"

"Tip a waitress? Whatevah fah?"

"Aha! Just as I supposed. Welcome to the party, Maine Redd."

I ducked down and gave him a good swipe across the knees with my 42s. Like any good Yankee, he yelled tersely. Out of the corner of my eye I could see Missouri Redd coming after me. I grabbed a handful of dirt as I stood and threw it in his eyes. He stopped and grimaced, and I gave him a left hook that almost broke my hand. He barely stopped to think about it; in fact, I might have just knocked the junk out of his eyes. It looked like my bag of tricks was empty, when a high-pitched voice from the porch said, "All right, you carnies, knock it off before I turn the hose on ya."

CHAPTER 12

California Lowball

"Who you callin' a carny, pee-wee?" Missouri Redd bellowed at Pinky Piscopink, who was standing with his hands on his hips looking like a wind-up toy. "I never worked a carny in my life!"

"A-yuh, he's rat," said Maine Redd, "if you don't count that tam with th' freak show, when you wuh playin' the 'Wild Man from Barneo' in that silly union suit."

"Don't talk about that," said his half-brother. "Those was days of . . . experimentation."

"I wouldn't give a rootie-patootie if you were flashin' your knobs in a cooch show," said Piscopink. "Although watching you two tough guys get bested by this over-the-hill joey has been mighty entertaining. Now, fly off somewhere. I wanna have a word with this guy."

"Who are you, Mighty Mite, tellin' us what to do?"

"We stahted this fat, and Ah don't think we've gotten ahr money's wuth yet."

"Take a rain check." The midget showed them his buzzer. "I'm not saying what you're doing here is such a bad thing, but I need to talk to him while his skull's still in one piece."

The two roustabouts turned their options over in their minds, which was at least as physically painful as the clem with me. How much trouble could a half-pint copper be? Then again, how tough would a midget have to be to make it as a cop, and a detective to boot? Since discretion is the better part of valor, the Redd Brothers thought it wiser to bring more guys the next time they ambushed me.

"All right, we're goin'," said Missouri, "but we're tellin' you, clown, quit doin' what you're doin', if ya know what's good for ya."

"If I knew what was good for me, I'd eat a vegetable every couple of months."

Missouri Redd wiped the blood off his upper lip with his hand. "Ya know what I'm talkin' about. Quit followin' people around. Get ya in big trouble."

"Land ya rat in the chowdah."

"Scram outta here, ya monkeys!" screamed Piscopink. The Redd Brothers left grudgingly, looking well practiced at it. Piscopink watched them, then hiked his hat back with his thumb. "Looks like I came in just in time. Those mugs were going to give you a permanent crease."

"I was wearing them down pretty well," I said, eyeing him carefully. "Another half-hour and they would've been begging for a rest."

"Yeah, you're welcome," he said. "Nice one with the mayor this morning, Koko. Oh, I was back in the crowd, only you couldn't see me. Brody better hope the papers don't run that photo with you falling asleep."

"Were you the token kinker, brought along to show how much the mayor cares about us poor show folk?"

"I'm not gonna dignify that with a response," said the diminutive detective. He unbuttoned his jacket and walked toward me slowly. "Of course, if he wants to improve his image, the mayor made another mistake in stopping you of all people, although I doubt the papers will bother to look it up."

I leaned back against a workbench and slowly lit a cigarette. "I don't know what you're talking about . . . detective."

He let out a rapid chuckle like a squirrel guarding his nuts. "Ah, that's a *hot* one," he said, as if this was all scripted for my maximum aggravation. When I didn't rise to the bait, he continued, "So, you've got a bad memory. Too bad. Mine's only okay. I couldn't place your name right away yesterday, but I didn't forget the face. Orange hair and all, I knew you were somebody. So I started asking around Top Town, to see if anyone could help me remember."

"So," I said, "after they sat down and bounced you on their knees, what did people have to say?"

Piscopink hopped up on a hay bale and smashed the cigarette into my face. "They told me smoking is dangerous," he snapped. "That it can cause big problems. That people *die* in fires."

He was clearly begging me to take a swing. Every part of me wanted to, but the only place that would do me less good than this blacksmith shop right now was the lock-up in Dukenfield, so I kept my cool. "You got it wrong," I managed to say.

"Oh? Everyone seemed pretty sure of it. The Great Charleston Fire. Mention that to anyone around here, and they'll just say two words: Rex. Koko. And is it just a coincidence that you've been hiding under floorboards for the past three years, and as soon as you skitter out into the open, a couple more kinkers drop dead? You go visit Berndt Bork, and his cannon suddenly misfires. You go see Flying Fleming, and his perch lurches. Yeah, I've got a couple of witnesses put you there last night. That's the trouble being famous, I guess: everyone recognizes you, even when you wish you were invisible."

My jaw clenched tight enough to give my leg a cramp. If it had been anyone else pelting me with this stuff, I probably would've stood there and taken it. Hell, a part of me might have even believed it. But this little hooligan was like a dose of ammonia salts, getting me off the canvas and swinging. You know how sometimes in the cartoons, they'll put a little angel on a guy's shoulder and a little devil on the other, talking into his ear? Usually, one or the other gets smashed like a bug. Well, here I was with a devil 10 times as big, right beside me. It was all I could do not to grab a shovel and use it like a flyswatter.

"You think you got all the answers, Piscopink? You got nanty. You got less than nanty."

"Wrong, clown. I got two murders and a patsy to pin them on. A blue plate special, served up nice and hot. I know you had something to do with Bork and Fleming. It won't be hard to figure out what, and then I'm gonna hang those murders on you. Life's cheap down here, you know that. Nobody cares about a couple of murders in Top Town, except me. When I put you away, all the other kinkers will owe me their gratitude, plus a few more negotiable benefits. My bosses will give me a commendation and less interference in doing my business. And I get the personal pleasure of sending a joey upstate for a date with the barbecue stool. Everybody's happy. Even you, I bet."

"Yeah, that would really make my day."

"Yeah, even you." He paused an uncomfortable amount of time, then said, in as low a voice as he could muster, "You want an end to this business, Koko. I can tell. Who wouldn't? All the whispers, the mistrust, the angry stares. No one wants you in Top Town, but you've got no place else to go. You want to quit remembering Charleston, and Walsh-Polansky. The fire, the smoke, the screams. You want it to go away. All out and over."

He looked at me as if goading me to be man enough to face the truth. All I could think of was the little cartoon devil, and how handy the shovel was.

"You think you got me under your thumb, Piscopink?" I muttered at last. "Ha! Your thumb is wedged somewhere else, nice and tight. I been set up and knocked down so many times I've got pinboys following me, but I'll become an insurance salesman before I let you get the best of me. I had nothing to do with those murders, and the fire is ancient history. Now, why don't you go find a tin cup and a nice organ grinder somewhere? I'm sick of your chatter."

"Count on it, Koko, I'm getting you for these," Piscopink barked, red in the face. "I got my eye on you."

"Well, don't get a crick in your neck," I said, as I walked out of the shop.

"Hey! Get back here," he peeped, "I didn't say you could leave."

I could hear the grunts as he climbed down from the hay bale, but I kept on walking. I lit another gasper and tried to calm down, but my hand was shaking like an Eskimo's Chihuahua. I didn't doubt that Javert Jr. was going to try every trick in the book to put me away. But what made me angrier was, he was pretty much right. I did want an end to things. An end to the suspicion, an end to the guilt. An end to the memories that haven't faded, that can be set off by anything from a horse's whinny to a balloon drifting away with no one to hold its string. I'd tried to drink them away, fight them away, laugh them away, but they're still there, fresh as new mushrooms. Short of doing a dry dive like Fleming, I guess they're mine for keeps.

But I still knew a few things Piscopink didn't, like how his every squawk urging me to give up only made me hell-bent to find the real killer or die trying. Seeing any kind of satisfaction on that man-in-the-moon face would be a fate worse than death. He also didn't know the connection between the stiffs and Carlozo. Okay, I didn't know much about it either, but at least I knew what I didn't know, but he didn't know what I knew and didn't know. He didn't even know he didn't know it, which was probably nothing knew.

I had to find Carlozo again, whatever the cost. A trip to the Hi-Wire was no more dangerous than waiting for more thugs to jump me. I could also pay Jimmy back for throwing me into the lamp post yesterday. But on the way, I had a stop to make.

I cut over to Adler Street and tried to get into Bork's back lot. His gate had been padlocked, so I found a lower part of the fence and climbed over. The place looked much the same as the day before. Everything seemed to be where it had been scattered or abandoned. Even his cannon mechanism was still there, untouched by the scavengers who were probably only biding their time. I pushed my way into his shack and pawed through all the debris in there. The place smelled of oil and sour milk. He'd kept it about as tidy as he'd kept his yard. It took almost 10 minutes of poking around, but I finally found what I was looking for: another queen of hearts, inscribed "Pierre 1928."

CHAPTER 13

Cutthroat

It was a little before 11. The leather doors of the Hi-Wire Lounge were locked shut. No surprise. The place probably opened closer to noon so all the lovely customers could get their beauty sleep. Since I had some time to kill before anybody showed, I went to the five-and-dime for supplies. Twenty minutes later, I came back and arranged a suitable welcome.

When I was finished, I waited on the stoop of the building across the street from the bar. Before long, the well-dressed figure of Jimmy Plummett came hustling down the street, slick as a cherry pit. He passed a few people on the sidewalk without a nod or a wave hello. When you spend your life kissing up to people flying above you, you don't spend much time looking down.

"THIS PROPERTY IS CONDEMNED."

The official-looking notice tacked to his front door made Jimmy do a perfect double-take. Squared off as if challenged to a fight, he preened his hair with the flat of his hand as he read. When he got to the fine print, which was nothing but synonyms for "sucker", he angrily ripped down the paper. Another was nailed to the door.

"AND FURTHERMORE . . ."

He ripped the second one down and found a third, which read: "You're standing on some, too."

Plummett looked down and saw sheets under his feet, this time with the shiny side up. Lifting one foot with the paper firmly attached, it finally dawned on him that the others were still stuck to his hands. He tried to flick them off, but the more he flapped and fluttered, the stronger they stuck.

I walked over slowly. "Morning, Plummett," I said. "Anything good in the papers today? Hoooohooo-hoooo-hooo."

The sound of my voice made him turn with a jerk. "Some gag," he snarled.

"I figured, what better way to catch a flyer than with flypaper? It may be too literal, but I try not to overthink these things."

"What are you doing here?" he asked as he tried to peel the sticky sheets from his hands. "Was I too subtle when I tossed you out yesterday?"

"Probably," I said. "I've got a pretty thick skull. Just ask the Redd Brothers. One of them broke his nose on it this morning."

"What are you yammering about?" he asked distractedly.

"The Redd Brothers. You know them: Big, grunt a lot, less hairy than bears..."

"So what?"

"So, somebody sent those knuckle-draggers after me about an hour ago, when I was supposed to meet Carlozo, and I'm guessing it was you."

He stopped his flapping and looked at me. After a beat, he said, "You're all wet."

"And you're all gooey. Look, I know you and I go way back—nearly 24 hours now—and we shared some intimate moments while you were shaving, but I still get the distinct feeling you don't like me too much. Maybe you sent the Redds to protect your pal, 'cuz he shouldn't be seen with the likes of me."

"I didn't send the Redds," Jimmy said. "I don't hang out with those kinds of characters, but smacking you around sounds like a good idea. We don't want you around, Koko. You trail disaster behind you like some kind of pushcart peddler."

"So you flyers are just going to circle the wagons and protect yourselves, eh? Didn't do Bork and Fleming much good. They're flyers with permanent wings now, and a harp and a halo to boot."

"They weren't flyers," he scoffed, as he continued to wrestle with the flypaper. "It's a shame they're dead and all, but I didn't know them. They were daredevils, not real flyers. I don't think either one of them ever came into the club, so your theory stinks."

"Oh, it may stink, or it may be pleasantly aromatic, but maybe you're just smelling your own memory. You did know Bork, because you were the one who introduced him to Boots Carlozo."

"And you heard that from her, I suppose? Boy, how stupid are they making clowns these days?"

"Stupid enough, don't worry."

Plummett tried using his teeth to hold onto the flypaper, but only got it stuck to his chin. "That broad is poison through and through. She's the one you ought to be asking these questions."

"Yeah, I'll get right on that."

"It's a shame Reynaldo ever married that bit of skirt. She's never been any good for him. The constant nagging, the vanity, the insane perfectionism . . ."

"She got in the way of all that?" I asked.

"AAAAGGHHH!" Plummett shouted in frustration. "Get these damn things off my hands! I'm begging you. I can't stand it!" Grudgingly, I reached over to his outstretched palms and with a quick yank freed him of the flypaper. He breathed a sigh of relief and out of habit ran his palms again across the sides of his head. Too bad they still had goo on them. When he realized it and pulled them away, he'd created a hairstyle that would've been quite chic down at the Peel.

Jimmy tried to collect himself with a few breaths. "You don't know about Reynaldo Carlozo. He's one of the greatest men I've ever known. Daring, dedicated. Fearless. Carlozo is the best trapeze artist I've ever seen. When he was up in the air, he made you think that that's where all men should be. He was more beautiful flying than most people are walking."

"Sounds like you have a crush on him."

"I've seen him fly hundreds of times. When I was younger, I tried to model myself after him, even though I . . . after my accident, I could never fly again. Still, I did my best to be like him, figured that . . . ah, forget it. What would a pie-tosser like you know about it?"

"I know as much as I want to," I said, "and believe me, it ain't much. Behind all this grace and daring is some kind of mania, which frankly always gave me the willies with you guys. And when that mania goes off track, look what happens. How do I know you didn't have a hand in the killings? He was your hero—maybe you wanted to get rid of his pesky wife and the embarrassment she was causing."

"Watch what you're saying, Koko," he said, his dander rising. "I stick up for my friends, but it doesn't go *that* far. Anyway, I've got alibis. I didn't leave the bar from opening til closing yesterday, and I've got a dozen people who'll back me up."

"All right, what about Pierre?"

"Pierre? What are you talking about?"

"What do you know about a guy named Pierre?"

"What, that he's French? The only Pierre I've ever known in the circus is long gone."

"Pierre Longhon? Where can I find him?"

"Not 'Longhon'. He's long gone. As in dead. Pierre Aubre, an acrobat, wire walker. He died on tour, probably 10 years ago. From what I know, he jumped into his net at the end of his act, and it gave way. Died a couple of days later, after a whole lot of pain." Jimmy reached over and rapped the telephone pole with his knuckles a couple times. "Yet another reason to stay clear of Boots Carlozo."

"How so?"

Jimmy looked at me like I was the dumbest cluck in the barnyard. "She was sleeping with him then."

"You're kidding me," I muttered.

"Don't you get it? She's a jinx, she's got the evil eye. Stay away from this whole mess before you end up with an anvil dropped on your head."

"You say that like it would hurt."

"Stick with your whoopee cushions, ace, and let the rest of us . . . get on with . . ."

Plummett was watching over my shoulder up the street. I turned to look, and saw Reynaldo Carlozo headed in our direction. "Looks like I can cut out the middle man now, Jimmy. Thanks for sticking around."

We turned and waited for Carlozo to make his way down the street. From his casual way of walking, I guessed he hadn't seen me or Plummett yet. He came up to the edge of the alley, when his path was blocked by a big, muscular gink. After a few words, he grabbed Carlozo and dragged him out of sight into the alley. Next to me, Plummett yelped like he was the one who got grabbed. We both ran over to rescue the flyer from his attacker, who was wearing dungarees and a checkered shirt.

CHAPTER 14

Texas Hold 'em

Plummett and I could hear the trashcans banging and pounding when we were halfway across the street. In the alley, Carlozo was being roughly fitted for a new necktie, with his attacker's big hands wrapped around his epiglottis. As I've said before, Carlozo was no dandelion, but this rust-headed wrangler was tossing him around with the greatest of ease.

As much as I wanted to savor the scene, the flyer's face had already turned red and was heading toward purple. I pushed my way between them and broke the young guy's grip. I tripped him and got him a little off-balance. Carlozo crumpled in a heap behind me, retching and gasping for air. I got ready to defend myself, only to realize that this guy had about six inches and 70 pounds on me.

"Y'best move along, clown," the young man drawled. "This don't concern you."

"You're right, sheriff, but I'm up to my neck in it anyway."

He was taken aback, either by my tenacity or my stupidity, then warmed up to the challenge. "I got no quarrel with you," said the cowboy, raising his fists, "but if you're wantin' a fight, I can set another place at the table."

"Don't worry 'bout me, Paw," I said, "I et before I come."

"Come on in the kitchen, pardner, I'll fix you up a nice knuckle sandwich."

"First, I need to ask," I said, checking over my shoulder, "is it kosher?" A right fist caught me on the jaw. "Owwww! Hey fellas, you wanna help with this? I'm running out of snappy metaphors."

Another right connected painfully, and I fell backwards over the cowering Carlozo. Fortunately, this gink forgot the first rule about fighting a clown: When you hit one, get ready for the bounce. He was leaning over to grab Carlozo again, when I found a foothold against the building wall, kicked off and sailed right at him. My skull hit his midsection hard and knocked him to the ground. Before he could stand, I grabbed him by the shoulders and climbed on top. I had his arms pinned under my knees, but surprise was the only reason he didn't toss me off like an old blanket.

"You wanna tell me why you were choking this guy here, or do I have to get funny?"

The cowboy was in his early twenties. He looked as innocent as a young peach, except for a jagged white scar running along his jaw line. "Get off, clown, or you're gonna get me good and riled."

"*That* must be a sight—you seem like such a reasonable fella. Carlozo! Who is this guy? Carlozo!" My inquiry was answered by the sound of his feet running down the alley. Jimmy Plummett stood there with his mouth hanging open, watching Superman run away from the bad guys.

"You better run, you skunk!" yelled the redhead. Without a glance or really much effort, he tossed me backwards into the trash cans and got up to look for the flyer, who by then was almost completely out of sight. Turning back to me, he said, "I don't know who you are, buster, but you oughta worry about who you're defendin'. Stickin' up for a polecat like that makes me take an instant dislike to you."

"I must say, you make a good first impression, choking a man in an alley like that. Studying for the ministry, are we?"

He looked at me like it was a straight question. "I ain't the studious type, but I know enough to stand up for what's right. Now you just stay outta my way, or you might get hurt."

"Thanks for the belated tip," I said, as I pulled my aching body to its feet. "Now, here's another trick question: What's the name of that little shack in San Antonio that everyone's supposed to remember?"

"'Little shack'?" His eyes grew wide as half-dollars. "You'd better not be talkin' about the Alamo, mister, or we're gonna have to throw down again."

I put my hands up in mock self-defense. "Pleased to make your acquaintance, Texas Redd. I had a little run-in with your brothers this morning."

"Half-brothers," he corrected. "I suppose you were doin' somethin' to rile them up, too."

"I think I was breathing too much to suit them." I was noticing something about this guy. While he was just as quick to anger, he didn't seem fueled by pig-eyed hatred like Missouri Redd. Something different was burning in him, something not entirely self-righteous, despite his preachy tone. "So tell me, Texas, what's your involvement with Boots Carlozo?"

"None of your business, clown, is what. And her name is Adeline, not Boots."

"You seem pretty interested in her."

"Meanin' what?"

"Meaning, she's seen you. She knows you're following her, as quiet as a dray horse. And if you've been following her, I'm guessing you know something about these murders. Either that, or you're just too shy to ask her to the Boll Weevil Cotillion."

I wanted to get a rise out of him, but he got one out of me—specifically, a rise to my feet off the pavement. His uppercut moved faster than I could see, and this time, I didn't bounce back. By the time I woke up, I was alone in the alley. I pulled myself up and looked to see if any body parts were lying around. Satisfied that my original equipment was battered but functioning, I picked up my hat and staggered across the street to the Hi-Wire. I pushed my way in and found Jimmy sitting at the bar, silently staring at the floor. The lights pointing up from his feet didn't flatter him. He looked like he'd just swallowed a fish that was none too fresh.

I walked around the back of the bar, filled a glass with ice, and poured a couple fingers of Canadian whiskey over it. I took a few extra cubes, wrapped them in a towel and held it against my lip. Jimmy said nothing, didn't even look at me.

"You really shouldn't have been so bashful out there," I said, taking a gulp of my drink. "There was plenty of that cowboy to go around. I would've shared."

Jimmy muttered, "Shut up."

"I will once my face swells up. But before that happens, you gotta come clean. This killing business isn't over. Tell me what you know, before somebody else gets it—Boots, maybe, or even Carlozo, the All-American track star. Or even me. I just know you'd hate to see your favorite whiteface punching bag make an early exit."

We were silent for a while. I helped myself to a fresh pack of cigarettes from a carton behind the bar and lit one up. Jimmy said, "I've got a place for you to go."

I took a drag and blew smoke into the harsh lights. "Anything to do with brimstone or pitchforks? Or cantaloupe? I'm allergic to cantaloupe."

"No," he said quietly. "You want some answers, you go to this poker game I know about and find them."

"Who's going to be there?"

"Depends. It's the biggest game in town. Run by Slats Kriehbel."

"Slats Kriehbel, the Armless Wonder?"

"That's the guy. They hold the game every night, up by the runs."

"Is this the same game where Bork and Fleming lost their shirts?"

He paused. "Just go up there and stir things up, see what you find out."

"Does it matter that I don't know how to play poker?"

Jimmy just laughed with that little whistle through his nose. Too bad I wasn't trying to be funny.

CHAPTER 15

Suicide King

Before this little tussle, Jimmy Plummett struck me as someone like an over-the-hill bally broad—indiscreet, insecure, trying way too hard to be liked. Not by me, of course. It was pretty sad to watch him act like the Mystic Kazoo of the Loyal and Exalted Brotherhood of Carlozo Fanatics. Redundant, too, since all flyers already carry around a rabid fan club inside their own heads. For all I know, it's essential to performing their daring feats, and when that interior fan club deserts them, the flyers hang up their tights before somebody gets hurt.

And now, Jimmy the bally broad had had his heart broken. After years of infatuation, adoration, and even emulation, upon reconsideration, his estimation fell from high elevation to annihilation. If I might make the generalization without, you know, getting condemned.

Carlozo ran from the rumble like a dog from a bath, his only defender yours truly. I'd expected a little more fight in him, but maybe beating up a sleeping, hungover joey is more his style. I'd almost feel sorry for Jimmy, except that he'd brought this disappointment on himself. Oh, and the fact that he was a Grade-A jackass.

If Jimmy's heart was broken, his might've been the only one I'd seen during all this. For all the spoiled romance, heated accusations, and—oh, I almost forgot—murder going on, not a lot of tears had been shed. Carlozo was pining for his wife like a piece of lost luggage, and the most Boots could muster in her grief was that her bunkies "didn't deserve to die that way." How they *did* deserve to die, I'm afraid to ask now.

Was it true about Boots and this long-gone Pierre, and if so, why'd she lie to me about it? Jimmy thought she was a black widow, but a guy like him probably thinks gremlins in the wire make a telephone work. What she'd gain from doing Bork and Fleming in, I couldn't see. It didn't make sense; it didn't even make nonsense, and I oughta know about nonsense. And what did I have now, aside from three Redd Brothers out of their cages, a married couple breaking down in public and taking others with them, and a vest-pocket detective who wants my tiny fedora for his wall, plus my head to hang it on? Nothing but an invite to a high-stakes poker game where I was a stranger—one where clowns probably weren't even allowed—with only $28 left in my pocket. So ask yourself, what would a reasonably cautious, rational, intelligent man do next? OK, now ask yourself, what would Rex do?

On my way up to the runs, I took a detour down to Hobie's newsstand. I was hoping the unflappable old geezer would calm me down enough to have second thoughts about this scheme. Hobie was also the one person that seemed to have no reason to lie to me, although maybe we just hadn't spent enough time together yet. As I headed down Grimaldi, I caught sight of his stand, nailed together from flimsy timber and old, discarded doors. He was sitting on a stool in front, the pages of the folded papers fluttering around him in the wind like the wings of pet pigeons. I didn't think I was being especially noisy, but when I got about 20 feet from the shack, Hobie turned and said, "What's the word, Rex?"

"The word is 'spooky'," I said. "How'd you know it was me?"

"Ah," he smiled, "you wouldn't ask a magician to give up his secrets, would you?"

"Depends on what he can tell me in return." With his grinning face pointed to the sky, I began to lay the spiel on Hobie, what had been happening and how I was in the middle of it. He patiently listened, puffing on his Lucky Strike, while I sorted it out for my own benefit as well as his. Hobie seemed to know everyone involved at least a little, even Piscopink. "I've had that little terrier come growl at me a few times," he said. "I can see one big mistake you made, son."

"Oh? What's that?"

"Taking Carlozo's money in the first place."

I lit a cigarette, feeling the pain in my jaw again. "Now it's my turn to play Sherlock Holmes," I sighed, "only I ain't English, I don't have an assistant to lob me dumb questions, and I ain't very smart."

Hobie thought a minute, then suggested, "You could always hire an assistant."

"Yeah, thanks," I muttered. "Why the hell am I doing this? Why don't I just wash my hands of this whole thing?"

"You would if you could," wheezed Hobie. "That's not your style. But just because you haven't solved this mess doesn't make you one of the bad guys. Cannon & Crowley, huh? I traveled with them once, back in the teens."

"Really? I never thought you'd . . . I didn't know . . ."

Hobie smiled, but was only a little amused. "Why else would I end up in Top Town, trying to sell something other than *Billboard* to you mokes? I wasn't born blind, y'know. Cannon & Crowley was a mighty fine outfit once."

"What else can you tell me about this Pierre guy? Why would anyone resurrect his memory? Or is he back from the dead, some voodoo hoodoo?"

"I don't know, Rex," he said. "That happened a long time ago. But let me point out the obvious: Two kinkers—maybe three—ended up dead after hooking up with Boots, and it wasn't from no jinx, no matter what that ninny at the Hi-Wire says. They were iced. And the guy she's married to is still alive. Now you say he's yellow. I would point out he's yellow and breathing."

"Yeah, but for how long?" I asked. "If Carlozo just wanted them dead, why pay me to come in and larry up his plan?"

"That's a puzzler, all right," Hobie said. "I tell you another thing. I wouldn't trust anything that oily barkeep tells you. Plummett's one of the biggest phonies around. Did you know, he ain't even a flyer?"

"What are you talking about?"

Hobie nodded sagely. "He passes himself off like one—for all I know, he might've convinced himself of it—but here's the deal: I could probably tell you every act that's gone out on every show for the past 20 years. I sit here all day and hear people's stories, and I've never found anyone who's ever performed with Jimmy Plummett. He may have done some acrobatics here and there, but he ain't never flown on no trapeze."

"But he runs the Hi-Wire," I said, incredulously.

"Hangin' out in church don't make you the pope."

"Nuts," I grumbled, grinding my cigarette out on the sidewalk. You think you know someone enough to hate him, and he pulls something like this. "One last thing: Tell me what you know about playing poker."

"Poker? Hey, what is this, a radio quiz?"

"There's one thing Bork and Fleming had in common—they'd both lost their leotards recently in the poker game run by Slats Kriehbel."

"Ah, that's no surprise," said the old man.

"Why not?"

"Aw, for years people have been grumbling that that game's not on the level."

"What are you telling me—the Armless Wonder is palming cards?"

"That's what I've heard. So, why do you have to know anything about poker? You're not going to play . . ."

"Sure I am. Can you think of a better way to get some information?"

"Yeah, 10 or 15 ways. It's just damned foolishness to jump into a high-stakes poker game—crooked or not—if you're no good at cards. You could end up broke, or broken, if you get in hock with them and can't pay. I don't even know if they'd let a clown in, to be honest."

"I'm not going to be honest, I'm going to solve this mess," I said. "If I jump into something over my head, that's nothing new to me."

"It's your neck, Koko, but you're sticking it out mighty far. For starters, what do you know about poker?"

"Eights are always wild, right?

CHAPTER 16

The Wild Widow

By the time I left Hobie's shack, my head was spinning like a pinwheel in a Kansas windstorm. What most gamblers learn during a lifetime of dissolute living, I was trying to gobble up in a single afternoon. Forget about mathematics and calculating the odds. It was all I could do to memorize the lingo. Full house, flush, straight, royal flush—in other words, a full house of tough customers, flush with cash, will go straight for the throat and wash me away like the king's morning stools.

But something in my gut told me to go play cards, whatever shook out. Jimmy might be as phony as the Feejee Mermaid, but watching his hero fall to earth took a lot of the starch out of him. He was sending me there to cause a ruckus, to get back at someone, but I wouldn't know who until I went. Going up to the runs may not have been the smartest decision I ever made, but it certainly wasn't the stupidest—not in the Top 10, even if you set aside drunken dares, impulsive tattoos and anything involving a live pig.

The clock hanging outside the Red Wagon Savings and Loan read 4:07. The game would be starting in about an hour. I had **60** minutes to figure out exactly how I was going to do this: how to get a half-dozen hardened gamblers to take me seriously enough to let me into their game to play poker to gain their confidence to tip their hands about what they knew about how two players from their illegal game met gruesome ends quite possibly at the hands of someone sitting in on the game at that very moment.

Impossible? Nah, I lied to myself. All in the timing.

I tried to think of what I owned besides a quick wit and a hard head that could get me through this stroll into the lions' den. In my trunk currently sitting under Lotta's protection, I had a spare coat with a few extra pockets sewn on the inside. Here was an opportunity. If I filled those pockets with a few extra decks of cards, and used all my digital dexterity to slip a few aces into the game, I could probably—let's say, *definitely*—spray the whole wad across the table, and they could bury me in the coat under the floorboards right there

I walked toward the Bimbo, trying to think of what else I had in my trunk that would help me. A few extra seltzer bottles, probably in need of a charge. A big wooden mallet, maybe good in self-defense. A cowboy outfit with fake riding ostrich. A Bombay horn. A giant pair of scissors. Not exactly an awe-inspiring arsenal.

Velda, hold the phone! There was one other thing in the trunk that might be useful, although I wasn't sure I'd have the guts to bring it. Tucked away in the bottom, wrapped in an oily rag, was a revolver I'd lifted from a belligerent townie in Michigan a few years ago. Why I still had it, I couldn't tell you. I never liked having it around, and had only fired it a couple of times for practice. But now might be a good time to have it with me, as long as it didn't go off in my pocket and shoot me in the interlude.

I cut down an alley off Fox and headed toward Griebling. A blustery wind puffed the sawdust into little cyclones at my feet. A change in the weather was coming, and if I could've felt my sinuses under my bruises, I might have had a headache.

As I passed a shadowy doorway, a low threatening growl made my neck-hairs stand at attention. Just what I needed, some idiot had let his panther run loose and bother innocent people. Really, those slangers ignore the leash laws whenever they feel like it, and then this happens. The important thing to remember in this kind of situation, especially for overweight joeys in size 42s, is to ignore the urge to run. If you run, you're rump steak. If you face the cat and hold your ground, it might remember its training and back down. I turned slowly, trying not to spook it. No such luck. A screech pierced the shadows, and before I could blink, I was knocked on my back, being clawed by a wildcat. A blonde one in a red bolero jacket.

I'd been in enough clems in the past two days to make a season of it, but fighting Boots might have been the worst. She was in a complete frenzy, blue eyes bugged out like a freak, trying to scratch, bite and kick anything she could. I would have socked her on the button to end it, but it was all I could do to protect my face and other vitals. She was taking hard swipes and slashes at my head as I wondered where I could get my hands on a whip and a chair. Suddenly, her expression changed from fury to surprise, and the color drained from her sweaty face. The punches stopped, and she straightened her body and kneeled beside me. Our eyes locked, and I waited for an apology, a confession, or a punchline. Then she turned and vomited on the ground next to my head.

I rolled out of the way—there's more than one type of self-defense—and watched dumbly as Boots emptied her stomach into the dust. She was pale and shaking, and when she was done, she lay down on her side and curled up like a kitten. Panting, she closed her eyes to rest, and before I could ask her anything, she passed out.

Boots was the first woman who ever lost her lunch from wrestling with me, at least that I could remember. While I didn't take it as a personal comment, I did reflexively check my deodorant. For a moment, I thought I should run, but I couldn't. Even though she'd looked happy to flay me alive, I couldn't leave her lying in the alley sick and passed out. I slapped her face a few times to rouse her, but she was out like Max Schmelling. She was too heavy for me to carry, so I sniffed around the alley and found a wheelbarrow. With great effort, I piled Boots in, covered her with a dusty carpet and wheeled her as inconspicuously as possible out of the alley.

On Griebling Street, a crowd of flatties was heading into the Club Bimbo to ease their minds with some bumps and grinds. Barging into the front door with a delivery of unconscious tomato was not going to work. I went around through the backyard and headed for the stage door. It was unlocked, so I bent over and with great effort hoisted Boots over my shoulder. I pulled open the door and carried her inside.

Backstage was busy, with musicians and stage hands running in every direction. It was almost showtime, but Lotta was nowhere to be seen. I pulled back a curtain over a doorway to my right, and lo and behold, discovered a sultan's harem of well-proportioned dames in their silks and skivvies. Man oh man, was it an eyeful. An earful, too—my surprise entrance sent some of them screaming like teenage banshees with a crush on Frank Sinatra.

"Take it easy, ladies, I'm just looking for a place where my friend can rest."

A big jill with chestnut hair came up and said, "Why you bringin' her around here? This ain't no flophouse."

"Ain't she got a home?" asked another.

"Well, see, she's my aunt, from out of town, and she wandered away from the church picnic, singing hymns and smacking her tambourine . . . and fell in with a bunch of teamsters brewing some moonshine . . ."

The big jill stood there with her arms crossed over her purple kimono, growing more put off by the minute. The pain in my back was getting unbearable.

". . . and dear auntie was so thirsty from singing . . . and . . . they started pounding drinks for every sin she could name that they'd cop to . . . and . . . and the moonshiners passed out or we'd still be there trying to save 'em and . . . and if I don't find a place to put her down, we're both going to collapse right here in the doorway, and you'll have to step over us the whole night."

"Hey, wait a minute," said another dame from the back of the room, "that's the joey who was bathing himself in the yard yesterday. He's a friend of the boss."

All the other jills took a sudden interest in my plight. "Is this the guy you were talking about?" asked one girl of another. "The one with the big . . ."

"Feet!" I said. "Big feet! And a big problem on my shoulders, honey, so if you could go get the boss and tell her Rex needs her help, I'd appreciate it."

The big girl in the kimono stepped up to me and said slyly, "If I take you to Lotta, will you come back to the yard and give us an encore performance?"

"Yeah, sure, glad to," I gasped. "Only find me a place to set down my . . . dear sweet auntie, or else I'm going to have a prize-winning hernia."

She walked up and unloaded Boots from my shoulders, got on the other side and helped me drag her body toward Lotta's office. Lotta wasn't there, but the jill let us in and went off to find her. I lay Boots in an armchair and carefully stepped back. She looked a little better but not much. This limp pile of laundry was the black widow? The curse of the daredevils? Pierre's bumper-offer? Not anymore. She was used up, spent. But I still needed to know she was in one place and would be here when I got back. Lotta would probably let Boots sleep here a couple hours securely while I went to the poker game. It was asking a lot of Lotta, but I was certain she'd be able to cut me this slack one last time.

At least, I was certain until I heard the door slam behind me, louder than a cement truck being dropped on a kettle drum factory. I turned and looked at my mountainous friend. "A funny thing happened on the way to the Bimbo . . . ," I began.

I'd seen Lotta mad before, but not this mad. It was like facing an open furnace with a gift for profanity. I'll skip the five minutes of nonstop bellowing. It was a little repetitive, very personal and not at all charitable. Besides, I don't think I could spell half the names she was hurling my way.

When she finally stopped to take a breath, I saw my chance and jumped in. "Lotta, baby, I'm not trying to wreck your business, or ruin your reputation, or anything like that. I just didn't have anyplace else to take her."

"So yew come round here draggin' an unconscious tramp through the place? How many of my customers want to see that?"

"Judging by the looks of them, I bet quite a few."

"Ah can't have this here in my club, Rex! We're barely making our nut as it is, and you come dragging around janes who belong in the gutter. Ah told yew this woman was trouble. Ah told yew to stay out of it all!"

"Lotta, listen," I said. "How much trouble can she be now? Maybe she's behind everything, and maybe she's not, but what can I do with her now until she wakes up?"

"Take her back to her husband, like he hired yew to. Or take her to the police. Just get her out of here."

"The bulls won't care about her. Ever since the first murder yesterday, I've had a midget cop latched onto my ankle. I'm the dope they want to pin this all on. Boots could be as bad as Lizzie Borden, for all I know, but I guarantee you, whether she is or not, they'll figure out a way to lock me up for sharpening her axe."

"Rex," she said, "how'd yew let this get so out of control?"

"Just talent, I guess."

For better or worse, that shut her up. In another part of the club, the band started their first number. Finally, Lotta asked in a concerned tone, "What's happened to her?"

I told her about the sickness, but played down our fight. It was a little embarrassing, after all, how many times I'd had my caboose kicked lately. "She's probably out for a while. You could just lock the door and get on with running the club, and when I come back in a couple hours, we'll let her out and I'll take her off your hands."

"A couple hours?" she asked, back at full volume. "Where th' hell are yew goin'?"

"I've got to find her husband," I said, which wasn't really a lie when you looked at it in the abstract and squinted your eyes. It was on my list of things to do, certainly, and would've been a great idea if I knew how to do it and where to start. Lotta was getting more flustered, but at least she wasn't throwing me out. "Lotta, trust me. Just stash Boots someplace in the club for a couple hours. She's not well, and I've got to know she's someplace safe. If she disappears again, I might too. You're my last chance here. You gotta help me."

I knew Lotta didn't think much of Boots, but I was counting on her better nature to take over. Finally, she looked me hard in the eye and said, "All right, Rex, as a favor to yew, she can stay. But only for a couple hours, and y'got to explain this all when yew come back. Ah got a cooch joint to run. Hiding things ain't what we do around here."

"Lotta, you're a life saver."

"And since Ah'm doing yew a favor, Ah expect one in return."

A new kind of fear grabbed me by the throat. "What kind of favor?"

She grinned like a 400-pound Cheshire cat. "Something of a more . . . intimate nature."

"That's the kind of favor I like," I lied.

Lotta leered at me. "Shall we make it, say, seven?"

"*Maybe* seven, if I eat a lot of oysters. More likely twice, with a footrub thrown in."

Lotta chuckled and reached over to pinch my cheeks. I was lucky she didn't see the sweat on my forehead. I may have dodged a bullet, but it looked like there was a cannonball somewhere in my future. She walked past me, picked up Boots with both hands and threw her over her shoulder as easily as if she were putting on a fox stole. "Ah've got a room with a couch for her," she said as she carried her out, "and better yet, a locking door."

My trip to this poker game was going to have to yield something worthwhile, or I'd have to take Lotta's name off my dwindling list of people to turn to. I was frankly amazed she was doing this for me. Lotta was really going above and beyond this time. Which made it that much more sickening for me to search for her cashbox in the desk and cloat $200 from it.

CHAPTER 17

Betting Against the House

Up by the runs was a very logical place to hold a poker game. Cheap rent, close to rail transportation, convenient yet removed from the public eye. You might think it a veritable garden spot, if not for the puppy-sized rats that hopped hither and thither across the steel rails shining in the late afternoon sun. I trudged across the cinders of this little Shangri-la, not quite sure if I should sneak up to the front door of the building or just walk over like I owned the joint. In my overcoat pockets, I could feel the weight of a full seltzer bottle on one side and my old revolver in the other. My stomach was doing pratfalls as I made my way to the low, windowless building. It looked like all the other shacks nearby—blue-gray, weather-beaten, surrounded by tufts of ragweed—except for the roadsters parked out front and the obviously sturdy front door. I walked up, stood on the front step and knocked. A small panel in the door slid open and a real tough mug stuck his face out.

"Yah?" he said.

I breathed deep and said in my raspiest voice, "I want in on the game."

"Ha," he said with no enjoyment. "What's the password?"

Password? Jimmy never said anything about a password! How many guesses was this goon gonna give me?

"I ask, what's the password?"

I thought for a moment and said, "It's a secret."

"Yah, it is."

"So let me in."

"Can't do that."

"So then, you're telling me it's *not* a secret?" I asked.

"I . . . I don't think so."

"Because, if it's not a secret," I explained, "then it's a pretty crummy password."

"No, no, you're right, it *is* a secret."

"Then let me in."

"Not til you tell me the password."

"I can't tell you that."

"Why not?" said the mug.

I leaned in close and whispered, "It's a secret."

"Oh, come on, tell me. I won't tell nobody else."

"All right," I said, "it's 'slumgullion.'"

"Who?"

"What are ya, deaf? 'Clove hitch'."

"No, that don't sound right."

"Sorry, pal," I insisted, "it *is* 'John Quincy Adams'."

"No . . . ah, nope, no . . ."

"All right, Professor, what do *you* think the password is?"

"'Anthracite'," he said proudly.

"Well, looks like we can't agree on that. Too bad. Sorry to bother you." I walked away from the door and heard the panel shut. I waited 30 seconds, walked up and knocked again.

The same mug answered the door. "Yah?"

"I want in on the game."

"Ha," he said again. "What's the password?"

"Anthracite."

The panel slid shut again and the door was opened. The mug gave me the once over, but couldn't place my face. I repeated the password to him nicely, enunciating every syllable. He motioned me through another door with a jerk of his thumb.

The back room was quiet and smoky and smelled of flop-sweat. For this I was thankful; it meant no one would smell it on me. Over to one side was a makeshift bar, just two chairs holding up a plank with glasses and a few bottles of hooch. A few gees were standing around the edge of the room holding up the walls, but the action was in the center, where a large, sturdy table sat. Around this were five players of various shapes and sizes. On a tall chair to the left, in a neat white shirt and slick black slacks, perched Slats Kriehbel, the Armless Wonder, cradling a red deck of cards in his feet.

No one looked up when I entered. Their attention was focused on the felt-top table littered with dollar bills and aloof pieces of pasteboard. "Excuse me, gents," I said, "is there room at this table?"

No one looked up. No one said anything.

"I said, is there room at this table?"

Kriehbel took a drag on his cig and muttered, "Not for a skid row pie-thrower."

"Aw, fiddlesticks," I said, "looks like I'll have to spend my inheritance money with the possum-back queens on Nock Avenue. At ten clams a throw, they'll probably kill me before I run out of geetus."

They still didn't look up. One player tossed some money in the pot with resignation.

"It'll take the undertaker twice as long to wipe the smile from my face," I kept at it.

Kriehbel dealt cards around the table and said, "Down and dirty."

"Hoo hooo," I said, "that's what I pay them for."

They continued their betting, ignoring me. I could feel the sweat seeping into my socks. If I pushed things the wrong way, the gorillas around the room would get to play with me like an old tire. But my mind was going blank, and a quick retreat seemed better than a quick funeral. "Well," I said as I turned to leave, "better go buy some lanolin before I hit the chippies."

A whoop of triumph erupted from one player at the table, with exasperated sounds from others. I was just about out of the room when I heard behind me, "Hey, clown, where do you think you're going?" I turned and looked. The gink who had just won was standing up and waving me back. "Get back in here! This is the first pot I've won in two days! You ain't leaving my side."

I walked over and made like I was happy for him. "Being a rabbit's foot is all well and fine," I said, "but I brought money to lose—I mean, play. I want a seat at the table."

The winner looked at Kriehbel, who gave the matter a little thought. The dealer had a long, creased, weary face that looked like he was trying to suck taffy off the roof of his mouth, but his dark glistening eyes were watching everything. He gathered up the cards with his feet, then motioned to the side with his head. "Grab a seat, laughing boy."

"Woohoohoo!" I said, still testing how much to play the rube. Being underestimated, unavoidable though it was, might come in handy. I crossed the room and eased up to my chair. "I really want to thank you fellas for letting me play, I really do, yessir," I said, as my posterior grazed the front of the chair, nudging it backwards and sending me sprawling on the floor. A natural reflex for me, one I should've nixed. The players were too preoccupied to find this funny, except for my new best friend, who was in such a good mood all of a sudden that he let out a good cackle.

As I gathered myself together and corralled the chair, Slats Kriehbel said, "You're welcome at the table for now, but keep the antics to a minimum. As in zero. Let's not distract from the dignity of the game." He cut the deck a few times with his well-manicured toes and shuffled it. "I assume you got the scratch." I reached into my pocket and pulled out the 200 bucks, plus the 20 or so I still had of Carlozo's money, and laid them in front of me. Kriehbel seemed satisfied and started dealing. "Stud, gentlemen."

"Oh, please," I demurred, "it's just a couple hundred dollars."

Kriehbel turned a pair of eyes on me as warm and friendly as railroad spikes. "Listen, pal, if you start turning this place . . ."

"'Stud'! Ha ha ha! 'Stud'!" roared the guy I was hexing. "That's a hot one!"

I looked to Kriehbel as if this was some sort of reprieve. He regarded both of us coolly. "If this becomes a problem, you will be booted without hesitation. Mr. Breen here does not run this game; I do."

"Then let's get going," said a fat man across the table, who I recognized as an old skinner named Hamms. "The joey's money looks good enough to me. Let's go."

While I know diddly-squat about poker, I've learned over the years how to read a crowd, even one this small. This bunch of mooks had been losing for a while, and they were tired of it. Dead tired. Frustration and anger buzzed in the air like horseflies, and like horseflies, needed something to bite. The most likely targets for stinging were me, Slats and whoever started winning a lot of money. This tricky business just got trickier.

"The game is stud poker. Ante up," said the Armless Wonder. His feet were pale and adorned with coarse black hair. They dealt the cards and handled the bills with a style most people couldn't duplicate with their hands. Kriehbel even wore a small silver band on one of the pinkies.

The game began again. Each man was dealt one card down, one up. My up card was a seven of spades; down, a four of diamonds. Next to me, Breen had an ace showing, so he kicked in five bucks. After another card from the dealer, I had a three of clubs. The bet was again to Breen, who now had two aces showing. When the last cards were dealt, Breen was sitting high with three aces showing. Fool that I am, I'm sitting to his right, with a straight.

Thankfully, three of a kind took a straight. At least, I thought it did.

"Call, gentlemen," said the Armless Wonder.

I flipped over my down card casually, to the sighs of the other players. Breen, who had been wearing a confident grin, looked a little crestfallen. Kriehbel said without emotion, "Take your pot, clown."

"What? Who? Oooh, well, ha ha, beginner's luck," I said, and even though I was sincere, it came across like a taunt. This was not the way to gain anyone's confidence. Losing effectively was going to take more care.

Kriehbel gathered up the cards and shuffled again. His graceful feet made me self-conscious about my enormous duck-stompers, which only seemed good for putting out fires and tripping charging rhinos. Then again, what was Kriehbel using his feet for but fleecing suckers? He wasn't a concert pianist or a heart surgeon, was he? For all I knew, he was probably a crummy dancer. Hell with him, I told myself.

The next game dealt was seven-card draw. Every player at the table stayed in til the end. I had two 10s as my hole cards, and at the end of five, had two 10s showing. If I took this hand, everyone would hate me, but I felt something like heartbreak at the thought of folding with four of a kind. Thankfully, Hamms was showing three nines, so I could quit without suspicion. But that was all Hamms had, and Breen won the pot with a spade flush.

Besides Breen and Hamms, two other guys were at the table with us, a wiry little guy with a goatee the color of rope and a big, pasty middle-aged guy with the complexion of a Norwegian mushroom farmer and the eyes of a trout. I didn't recognize either of them. "Ha ha," I said, as heartily as I could, "this reminds me of a funny story I heard from my friend Pierre. Ha ha. Any you fellas know Pierre?"

Not a peep. You'd get more conversation from that painting of the poker-playing dogs.

"No? Well, anyhoo, Pierre was complaining about the price of make-up these days—he's a bit of a *queen,* y'see—and Pierre was saying a regular tube of foundation cream costs $19.28. Wowee! Can you believe it? Nineteen twenty-eight, that's right, Pierre, nineteen twenty- . . ."

"Listen, clown," said Kriehbel, "if you insist on flapping your gums like this was a garden party, I'm going to have you escorted out by Lester here. He could use the exercise."

I made a motion to lock my lips shut and throw away the key, which satisfied him. Kriehbel dealt two more games of Texas hold 'em, and Breen won them both. I've seen better winners, but this guy seemed to be coming off a long dry spell. He laughed too hard with relief, like this money was going to give Grandma her life-saving operation, or rescue her from loan sharks. He kept saying things to me like, "You're my rabbit's foot" and "Never leave my side, clownie." Which calmed me down not a bit.

"Say, you guys hear about the accidents yesterday?" I said, trying to sound casual again. No one picked up on it. "Pretty gruesome, I'd say. And two in one day? Who'd a thunk it? Wonder if they had family or anything. Or knew any Frenchmen from, say, 15 years ago. Who might be dead now. Or maybe not."

No one's face showed the least interest in what I was saying. Kriehbel had dealt spit in the ocean, and the guys were intent on counting cards. I hadn't checked my cards but tossed in the pot anyway. "Anybody know those kinkers? Bork and Fleming? The Human Howitzer? Seems like they'd been around town awhile . . ."

"What did I tell you about the chatter?" Kriehbel asked.

"I saw them both," I said, "just before they went south. Well, Bork went more south by southeast, if I were to guess, but you know what I mean . . ."

"I'm warning you," said Kriehbel, pointing a toe at me.

"Shut up and deal the cards," said the goateed geezer, with too much edge in his voice.

Everyone's eyes darted around the table. Kriehbel dealt to the players but kept his eyes glued on me. I tossed two cards down and got two new ones. Intending to bet a dollar, I grabbed a 10 by mistake and threw it in. I was surprised as anyone—I didn't even know what I had in my hand. My gulp was so loud it echoed in the room.

Breen gave me an incredulous look. Was the genie now bluffing Aladdin? Which way should he bet? Was it a set-up? He tossed in his sawbuck, and was followed by Hamms, the old goat and the mushroom farmer. Santa's workshop wasn't any colder than that back room just then. I wanted to call, I really did, but instead I threw in another 10, to the exasperation of everyone present. Sorry, Ma, this was not a friendly game of poker.

Everyone kicked in again, and the gee with the goatee called. The wild card on the table was a four. I looked at my hand: One four and three queens. I laid them down gently, as if they would explode on impact. "Err . . . five queens?" I squeaked.

Lord love a clown, because no one in that room did. Angry snarls erupted around the table when everyone threw down their cards in disgust. Breen turned to me with a crushed look in his eyes. The old goat pointed at Kriehbel and said, "What are you pulling this time, Slats? You trying to break us or something? It wasn't enough to squeeze those flyers, now you're trying to bleed *everybody?*"

"You watch your mouth, Otto!" shouted Kriehbel, as the trouble boys in the shadows began to stir themselves. He turned to me and said, "This is why I don't like clowns in my games. You're pulling something. Take off that coat."

"Please," I said, all coy, "I do have my dignity."

"Take off that coat before we rip it off you."

He wasn't kidding, but I could tell Otto the Goat wasn't kidding about Kriehbel, either. Something was more than fishy here, it was positively oceanic. "Okay," I said. "Good thing I washed my cuffs this morning." I stood up slowly and emptied my pockets: seltzer bottle, joy buzzer, popcorn ball, leftover flypaper. I didn't bring out the gun, because I didn't want to see if anyone else had brought theirs.

"Take off your coat!" yelled Kriehbel. I could feel rough hands on my collar. I ducked down fast and fell out of it to the floor, so the tough guy was left with all clothes and no clown. Chairs scraped and tipped over. I crawled to the side and got to my feet again, and watched Otto reach across the table to grab Kriehbel by the ankles. He pulled the Armless Wonder across the table and onto his back. Kriehbel was startled, but soon had a leg free and was winding up to give Otto a roundhouse kick to the head. He missed, and Otto flipped him onto his stomach and reached up Kriehbel's pant leg. There he found a few hidden aces and kings Kriehbel was saving in his garter for his own purposes.

The palooka next to me didn't know whether to grab me or rescue Kriehbel, so I took my seltzer bottle, swung it up and caught him under the jaw. Glass and fizz water sprayed everywhere, but he was out. Breen reached for me, but I spun the unconscious, teetering slab of beef around and pushed him between us. Otto and Kriehbel were still wrestling on the table, and Hamms was getting in on the act. Another torpedo made to grab me, but I took the sheets of flypaper and upholstered his face. Handy stuff, that flypaper.

Always looking for the perfect exit, I snatched my coat, grabbed my money from the table (including the pot, which I'd won, you know, even if Kriehbel had forced it on me), and tried to make a dash for it. But blocking the doorway was the pasty-faced farmer who hadn't said a word the whole time I was there. He gave me a look with those wet fish-eyes of his. "You can't leave with all our money," he said.

"Watch me. I won this money fair and square."

"But if you run off, I won't be able to make my payments."

"On what? The family tractor? The mushroom barn?"

The man looked at me puzzled. "What are you talking about? My flugelhorn is in the pawn shop, and I've got an audition with the Spaulding Sinfonieta on Thursday. If I don't get it out of hock, it means years of schooling down the drain, plus a broken-hearted mom. So, in the name of the arts, fork over the dough, clown, or I'll turn you inside out."

"Come and get it, Beethoven," I snarled. "If I can save the world from affliction by one single flugelhorn player, I'll have done my duty." The budding virtuoso lunged and gave me an uppercut that rang my glockenspiel. With rocks like those at the end of his arms, I pitied whatever instrument gave this guy trouble. He landed another punch that sent me to the floor. But as he reached for me, I scooted through his bowed legs, quick like a cockroach. I flipped on my back and, as he turned around to face me, kicked up and gave him a taste of my 42s between the legs. The wet look in his eyes gained a remarkable focus as he fell to his knees, then rolled to the side. Kriehbel may have had a surgeon's feet, but I was never more happy for my own boats than just then. I crawled through the outer room, burst through the door, and hit the cinders running.

CHAPTER 18

Tip of the Hand

By the time I got back from the runs, a rollicking night in Top Town was already underway, with calliope music steaming up the streets, light bulbs flashing above and below, and spielers using every verbal trick they knew to separate the suckers from their spondulicks. But it was all lost on me. I ran to the Club Bimbo as fast as my legs would spin, imagining all the players from the game chasing me on horseback with whips and machetes. While scared for my life, a part of me was pleased with my performance. I'd beat the odds there in more ways than one. I'd also learned that Bork and Fleming had been skinned on purpose. Money's nice to have, so I'm told, but it made no sense for Kriehbel to ruin two regular players. You don't kill a cow that still gives milk. So if busting them flat made no monetary sense, he must have done it for other reasons. Some kind of revenge? Hatred? To make an example of them?

Maybe Kriehbel just wanted those kinkers out of his game. But no way were the bankruptcies and the murders coincidences. While the Armless Wonder could do a number of amazing things, climbing Fleming's ladder and gaffing his platform wasn't one of them. Something bigger was going on, but the game hadn't showed me what. Likewise, if anyone there had any dope about Pierre, my subtle interrogation techniques failed to pry it out of them.

Once at the Bimbo, I snuck through the same stage door I'd en-tered a few hours before. Backstage was pretty vacant; everyone must have been onstage for a big number. I could hear the hoots and whistles of the customers and the grunts and shrieks of the girls onstage (the Bimbo prided itself on having, if not the prettiest girls on Griebling, at least the most flexible and inventive). Lotta wasn't in her office when I pushed open her door. Slipping inside quickly, I put the 200 bucks back in her cashbox, plus two sawbucks for her troubles. I'd explain it all later, or try to. This left me with a $118 in bunce from the game, not bad for someone who didn't know a straight flush from freight slush when he woke up this morning.

Suddenly I froze. Despite the audience pounding on the tables and the blood pounding in my ears, the whoop of Lotta's voice from the hallway came through loud and clear. I ducked under her desk and made myself as small as possible, praying she wouldn't come in the office. But she did, and closed the door behind her. Worse yet, she pulled out her desk chair and sat down. Lotta sat there silently for a half minute, then let out a sigh that set the lampshades rattling. I heard a little whimpering sound, which might have been crying. Then the telephone clanged like a fire station bell. After a couple more nerve-shattering rings, she picked it up.

"Yeah? . . . what do *yew* want? . . . Ah already told yew t' quit calling me about it . . . Ah ain't even going to discuss it, the answer is still no . . . Ah don't care, bring him over, Ah'll take both yew on . . . Call me again, and Ah'll come over and break yore handsome neck, sugah . . . and yew *know* Ah will."

The tone in Lotta's voice would've made a mad dog reconsider his options. I knew she was forceful; I'd heard her in action in business before. But there's forceful and then there's forceful. Taking that $200 may have been stupider than I'd thought. Lotta slammed down the phone, and we sat there in silence. I held my breath and tried to blink more quietly. That ended when Lotta reached under the desk, grabbed me by the throat with one hand, and hoisted me out into the open like a rabbit from a hat.

"Who the hell is under . . . REX!?" she bellowed. "What are yew doin' under there? Trying to see London and France?" She pulled me close to her unsmiling face. "Or is it something a little less wholesome?"

As charmingly as I could, I explained, *"Chkkch-kkczzz-khk-chkxxx . . ."*

She continued with a tight grip. "It's a mean, ugly world when old friends can't trust each other. When was it Ah cleaned yew up and gave yew breakfast? Wasn't it just yesterday? And yew bring yer girlfriend around here with a song and dance, and expect me to play mother hen? Then money goes missing from my office, and the competition starts to put the screws to me . . ."

As her voice grew shriller, her grip on my throat got tighter. If this kept up, I was going to need a ladder to put my hat on. I tried swinging at her, but all I could hit was the skin flap hanging under her arm. As spots began to dance before my eyes, I rummaged in my pockets for a biscuit I'd taken from the Pie Car that morning. I began to wave the dusty snack in front of Lotta's eyes, then tossed it to the side. She had to use both hands to catch it, so she dropped me on the desktop. I did a quick backwards roll and landed on the other side of the desk. I was safe for the moment, unless she wanted honey.

"Hold on a minute, Lotta," I said in a new, squeaky voice. "No need to get rough. I'll admit, I borrowed the money, but it was only for a short time, and I was just in here to pay it back, with interest, no less."

"Liar!" she shouted, spitting crumbs.

"Look in the cashbox. It's all there. You know I wouldn't steal from you, unless there was a good reason, or it was just lying around uncounted. I had to force my way into a big poker game, but I needed more than cigarette coupons."

At this, Lotta's anger subsided a little. "What poker game? Yew don't play poker."

"I didn't until just this afternoon," I bragged. "And I made a tidy sum. If my luck holds like this, I think I'll invest in some oil wells before I know too much for my own good."

"Yew didn't . . . it wasn't Kriehbel's game, was it?"

"You bet. The Armless Wonder himself."

Lotta collapsed into her reinforced chair. "That's it, then," she sighed. "It's all over. That's why Plummett called me."

"Plummett? What's that lounge lizard got to do with you?"

She looked at me with a look of affection like you might give a little bip who'd spilled ink all over himself. "What's it like, Rex, to go through life so stupid?"

"Oh, I don't know. Better than being a lawyer, I suppose. Thanks for asking."

"Why the hell did yew go up there?"

"Information. What do you know about Kriehbel?"

Lotta sighed. "More than anyone should, sugah. Just the mention of his name gives me the willies."

"Because he's a card cheat?"

"That's part of it. The other part is, Ah've played his game too much."

"What, you gamble?"

Lotta nodded. "Big time. In case yew hadn't noticed, Ah've got a problem with impulsiveness. And Ah've been losing too much to him lately. If Ah don't stay away from him and keep my nose to the grindstone, Ah'm going to lose everything Ah've got."

"How deep are you into him for?"

She paused, as if waiting for the answer to come from someone else. "Eleven grand. Ah've already signed away part of the Bimbo."

119

"To Kriehbel?"

"Rex, Rex . . . open yore eyes! Who do yew think Kriehbel works for? Who do yew think bankrolls him and gives him the gunsels to protect the game? That operation, and many another shady deal in Top Town, is run by T.C. Montgomery."

"Montgomery? That little leprechaun? Now he's your partner here?"

Lotta's lip trembled and she looked down at the desk, ashamed. "Yeah, 'partner.' He also owns the Hi-Wire, which is why Jimmy Plummet's been calling me, taunting me about how he's going to take over my club eventually, so why don't Ah sell it now while Ah can still get something for it."

"Looks like they've got you over a barrel, Lotta," I said in sympathy, "which is no mean feat, when you think about it. So Montgomery runs the poker game *and* the Hi-Wire? Jimmy must've sent me there knowing I'd bust the place up."

Lotta shook her fists and gave out a choked scream of frustration. "Oh, Rex, Rex. Ah'm so sorry, Ah let you down."

"I'm glad you let me down, actually—you were about to pinch my head off my neck. Wait a minute! Lotta, is Boots still here? Where is she?"

She choked a little. "Ah'm sorry, Rex. Maine Redd and Missouri Redd came here while yew were gone. Ah couldn't stop them."

"Where'd they take her?" I shouted.

"Ah don't know, they wouldn't tell me. Ah couldn't stop them, Rex. They're animals. Ah hope the poor li'l thing's all right."

There was a look in Lotta's eyes I'd never seen before, worried and wistful at the same time. "'Poor li'l thing'?" I asked. "For two days, you've been talking about her like Typhoid Mary, and now she's a 'poor li'l thing'? What gives?"

"A bit after yew left, Ah went to check in on her," Lotta explained. "She'd woken up, but still looked bad. She wanted to talk, so Ah listened. She was all panicked about some red-headed cowboy who'd been following her and tried to grab her."

"Yeah, I know who she's talking about."

"She's so worked up that Ah need to calm her down before she claws the paper off the walls. With the murders and this cowboy and everything else, she's just hangin' by a thread. Then, on top of that . . ."

"Yeah, she goes and gets sick."

Lotta corrected me. "She ain't sick, Rex. She's in a delicate condition."

"Delicate? I was lucky to survive meeting her."

"She's expecting a baby," Lotta patiently explained.

"C'mon, who'd trust her with their kid? Not to judge, but she's a little less than reliab—" Lotta threw a paperweight and hit me square on the head. "Oh, her own baby. Right, got that. Wh—EXPECTING A BABY!? WHO? WHEN?"

"Ah don't know any more, really," said Lotta sadly, "because just then, those two filthy roustabouts busted in and took her away. Aw Rex, y'gotta do somethin' to help that kid."

I put my head in my hands and squeezed. The Redd Brothers could have taken her anyplace—they probably wrote the route card on crummy hiding places around town. But they found her here in the first place either because they followed me and the wheelbarrow, or guessed I'd bring her here. And the only person who saw me here yesterday besides Lotta and the girls was Montgomery.

"Lotta, get Montgomery on the phone," I said. "Those goons were sent here by your 'gentleman' partner."

Lotta looked at me and did as I asked. Her plump hands danced on the black dial like little pigs feet. No one picked up on the other end.

"Try calling Plummett back at the Hi-Wire."

She did, and as it was ringing, handed the blower across the desk to me. A soft voice trying to sound hard said, "Talk to me."

"Hey Plummett, this is Rex Koko."

"Ah, the famous clown detective. Do me a favor and lose my number."

"I'm looking forward to it. The day I forget your number will be one that I'll never remember."

"Yeah . . . what? Listen, blockhead, things are busy over here . . ."

"I'll let you get back to your ladle and bathtub in a minute," I said. "I just got out of the poker game."

There was a little whistle of amusement on the other end of the line. "So, did they skin you alive?"

"Not exactly, although I had to leave the place in a hurry."

"Did you learn anything?"

"Never play cards with someone with less than one hand," I said. "Also, Kriehbel had clipped Bork and Fleming. Left 'em flat broke. Why would he want that?"

"You gotta . . ."

"No, scratch that. Why would T.C. Montgomery want that?"

Jimmy paused. "That's the question, ace. Sorry I don't know the answer. I truly don't. Out of curiosity, how'd you leave the game?"

"In a shambles," I said, "and with a nice profit." Jimmy whinnied again. "Listen, you gotta tell me one thing, and tell it to me straight: is Boots Carlozo over there?"

"No."

"What about her husband?"

"He's not here. either. He actually showed his face a little while ago, but he left in a hurry."

"I think you hero is in danger. If you tell me where he went, maybe I can stop it."

There was a pause, and the old Jimmy reemerged. "You're fulla hay, clown. You're a bigger danger to him than anyone in town."

"And you're a superstitious old scrubwoman. Boots is in the soup, too, snatched up by the Redd Brothers. Now tell me where he went before anyone else gets hurt."

Another pause. "The Plew factory."

"Why would he go down there?"

"I don't know. Sometime today, an envelope was dropped off here with his name on it. When he opened it, there was a note telling him to go to the Plew factory, and when he read it, he tore off outta here."

"Was there anything else in the envelope?"

"Yeah. A playing card. Queen of hearts."

CHAPTER 19

Ace in the Hole

As any old salt in a seaport can tell you, you need room to stretch out if you're going to sew a canvas. So the only place in Top Town with enough space for a sail loft like the Plew Perfect Tents factory was over in the flats at the east end of town. I gave Lotta instructions on how to divvy up my estate—a depressingly short explanation, I'm sorry to say—and after a kiss and a "break a leg," I hightailed it out of the Bimbo down Slivers Street. The wind was blowing hard, making the trip feel like it was all uphill.

The Plew Perfect Tents factory had two distinct halves, one three stories tall, the other single-story, long and wide. For all I knew, Montgomery owned this place, too, as well as the Pie Car, the Monkey Hostel, Bingo's pants and all the tea in Tijuana. Two globe lights lit the battered, faded sign on the building's front. The main entrance was secured with a heavy chain and padlock. Apparently I wouldn't be able to just saunter in blithely and get myself killed. I sneaked around the tall side of the building looking for another way in.

"Looks lahk Ah can take that rain check nah," said a voice behind me, frighteningly close. I tried ducking to the side, but something came down hard on my shoulder. The burning pain turned my right arm into sauerkraut. Lucky I'd moved a bit, though, or it would have been my head. Before my attacker could wind up again, I spun with my good elbow out, hoping to make contact with something vital. This threw me off-balance, and he caught my foot with his and tripped me up hard. Before I knew it, I was on my back with him on top of me.

"Sorry, Maine," I said as we struggled, "the box office is closed."

"But Ah've got m'ticket right heah." He swung an iron strap at me that almost tore my ear off.

"Show's over," I said, trying to shift his weight off me. "Try tomorrow, sonny."

"But Ah want m'show rat now, befah y'sneaks aff." He raised the bar again to split my skull, but I gave him a hard jab in the armpit. That pause was all I needed to reach around and kick him on the side of his head. My 42 landed flat with a good smack, and Maine Redd called out as his eardrum got the Gene Krupa treatment. Then I pushed him off and got out from under.

"So you think I'm the type to cut and run, you Yankee pot roast?" I asked, as I wrestled him for his club.

"Well, y'wuz *actin'* like y'wanted some tough-guy bantah, so . . ." A knee to the solar plexus cut him off.

"If I did, I'd've chosen a better theme!" I pried the piece of iron out of his hand and gave him a good thump on the temple. He wasn't squirming much after that. I felt the ear that Maine had hit, and saw blood on my fingers. An inch from disaster. Par for the course. On the bright side, I knew I was at the right place. If either Texas or Missouri got the jump on me, it might mean the big blow-off for yours truly. But I'd come this far, put friends in danger, made new enemies, got myself in hot water with the cops and the mayor, and possibly booked a romantic rendezvous with the former World's Daintiest Fat Lady. Can't close ahead of paper now.

Panting like a sick dog, I searched for another way into the sail loft. On the far side was a loading dock with a sliding barn door partially open that I squeezed through. It was as dark inside as it was outside, but I followed what lights I could find. They led me to a staircase, which I snuck up quickly. The door of the second floor was locked, but the third floor was wide open. Through the door was a short hallway, at the end of which was the door to a cavernous room, lit feebly with a few lamps hanging from the rafters. The wind outside howled through the big dusty space and chilled it like a meat locker. Voices were coming from the room, so I peeked around the corner.

In the middle of the room stood Carlozo, with his back facing me. His figure was unmistakable, but there was something different about the way he held himself. His legs were set apart, his broad shoulders hanging low. He was either ready to deliver a blow or recovering from one. Also in the room was that boiled hambone Missouri Redd, standing with his arms crossed over his dirty overalls. Standing next to him, looking especially pleased with himself with his Homburg hat and walking stick, was the bearded figure of T.C. Montgomery.

Now was the time to do something—call the cops, stampede the horses, do a Tarzan yell—*something*. But while I considered my options, Montgomery yelled, "You may come out into the open, Mr. Koko. We know you're there."

"Oh yeah? How do you know?"

"Because . . . you just answered me?"

He had me there. I entered the doorway, but went no further. Yellow and crimson canvases hung behind the men across a cable, giving this all the feeling of a sideshow. "We also heard you clomping and tromping up the stairs," smiled the old man. "Really, for sneaking around, you might as well have been wearing a cow bell."

"It's in my other coat. What's going on here?"

"In due time, sir," he said. "I first want to acknowledge, here in public, that your tenacity surprises me. Shocks me, even. You bounce around more than a rubber ball. No matter how hard you get smacked down, you come back for more."

"Comes with the shoes."

"My plans were laid out so precisely, and then two days ago, Mr. Carlozo brings you into the picture. The comic relief is a pleasure, if short-lived. I'm a little perturbed, however, that you decided to drop in on my poker game. It's been going a long time, quite profitably, but now that's over. I'll have to shut it down and establish it somewhere else."

"Real estate doesn't seem to be a problem with you, Montgomery," I said, edging forward a bit, "the way you seem to be throwing your muscle all around town. Oh, speaking of muscle, I left one of your bonny boys lying in the dirt downstairs. I don't think he's dead. It was easy to get the jump on him. That's one reliable thing about fighting Maine Redd: he'll always fall for a cheap shot."

Missouri Redd moved forward to give me what he'd call a wallopin', but Montgomery stopped him with a hand to the chest. "Yeah, and I already bested this galoot with his brother this morning. Two against one, and they still couldn't put me down. And then a *midget* made them hit the road. With muscle like this, Montgomery, it's a wonder you can get your car washed."

"All right," barked Carlozo, in a voice that commanded respect even in this empty warehouse, "enough of this! You brought me here, now what do you want? What do you want with me?"

"Reynaldo, old friend," Montgomery purred, "I wanted to relive some old memories with you. Cut up some jackpots, as it were."

"I don't know you from Adam," said the flyer angrily.

"Oh, but you do, Reynaldo. We go way back. Just think about it. The Cannon & Crowley show."

I edged into the room a bit more. Carlozo's face was a knot of concentration, while Montgomery tried to suppress an excited, clattering grin. "That miserable mudshow?" the flyer asked. "Bah! A low point in my career. While I may have blocked some of it from my mind, I don't remember you. Not at all!"

"I'm hurt," Montgomery said mockingly, "but not surprised. Think back, to South Dakota."

Carlozo paused, more confused by the minute. The hanging canvases waved in the drafty air slowly. "South Dakota?"

"South Dakota," I chimed in. "Oh, I remember that place. Flat. Very flat. Kinda dry. And flat."

"To be more exact," said Montgomery, "Pierre, South Dakota."

"I'm peering at it in my memory right now," I said, squinting. "What am I supposed to see?"

"Not 'peer', you idiot—Pierre."

"'Not peer—peer'. Are you listening to yourself, old man?"

"The Pierre in South Dakota," he said angrily.

"Oh come on. I'm sure there's more than one pier in South Dakota. It may be dry, but there's gotta be places . . ."

"Hey!" shouted Missouri Redd, now pointing a heavy black pistol at me. "Be quiet, yer makin' my head hurt!"

Montgomery took a deep breath, trying to stay calm. "The capital of South Dakota is spelled 'Pierre'," he said slowly, "but it is pronounced 'peer'."

"What th' . . . really?"

"Yes, really."

"That's crazy."

"Perhaps, but . . ."

"So the Pierre on the playing cards is . . .?"

"Yes!"

"And not a . . .?"

"Yes!!!"

"Oh," I said. "I'll have to call that fella at the French Embassy and apologize for badgering him."

"Yes," said Montgomery condescendingly. "Now, to get on with . . ."

"Treat him to a *bierre* sometime," I mused.

Montgomery raised his cane and despite his gimpy leg made a move toward me. Carlozo stepped in between us. "Leave him alone. If you have a beef with me, let's hear it. I still don't know what you're talking about with all this South Dakota nonsense."

A squealing noise came from behind the striped canvases billowing behind Redd and Montgomery. "What was that? Are there more rats in this place than just you two?"

"Far from it, clown," said the old man. "That was just the last player to be heard from. Someone who is going to make this all the more interesting. Missouri, wheel her out, please."

The roustabout slipped his pistol into the bib of his overalls. Carlozo kept looking at Montgomery, trying to figure out who this guy was. Missouri Redd lumbered over and pulled aside a section of canvas like a curtain. The light made it hard to see what he was doing, until he emerged again, pushing a deskchair on wheels in front of him. Tied to the chair, with a festive gag over her mouth, was the furious figure of Boots Carlozo.

CHAPTER 20

No Peekie

Watching Missouri Redd tiptoe around Boots was hilarious. Judging from the fresh scarlet scratches on his cheeks, the big roughneck had had as much trouble with Boots as I did, and he was clearly afraid that our favorite hellcat could bust out of her ropes at any moment and turn him into hamburger. There was no sign of fear in her eyes. Just cold resignation, along with a determination to break free if given half a chance. But those ropes looked pretty snug. If there's one thing a roustabout ought to know, it's how to tie some knots.

"What's the meaning of all this?" snarled Carlozo slowly. "Why are you doing this to my wife? Let her go this minute."

"No, no, not possible," said Montgomery with a slight but eager smile. "She's an important part of the game."

"GAME? What the devil . . ." Carlozo started toward the old man, but Missouri Redd intervened with his bulk. "What 'game' are you talking about? Why are you doing this to me? What do you want from me?"

"Me, me, me," Montgomery mocked. "Always about me. Your ego is still astounding, after all these years. Your wife's life is on the line, and your main concern is yourself."

"You . . . what kind of coward ties a woman up like this?"

"Carlozo, don't presume to lecture me about cowardice . . ."

"Nanny-nanny-boo-boo," I said. "Quit with yer taunting already. It's starting to feel like a schoolyard around here— I'll explain what that means later, Mizzou." The roustabout casually snorted and spat, hitting the space between my feet like a sharpshooter. The split lip I gave him earlier was no handicap to such a professional.

"Be that as it may," Montgomery continued, "one of the reasons we are here tonight is the fact that Reynaldo Carlozo does indeed possess enough ego for 50 normal men. This is the genesis of this entire saga. It's no surprise he doesn't recognize me, not at all. But we do know each other, Carlozo. We do have history. Think back to 1928. What were you doing that year?"

"Not until you untie my wife."

"In 1928, you were with the Cannon & Crowley Circus Sensational," Montgomery said, his dentures clacking away. "In fact, you were the headliner, the star attraction. But two other men were flying with you that year. Do you remember who they were?"

"They didn't fly with me," he scoffed. "I don't share the bill with daredevils whose only talent is to blow themselves into space. Where's the skill in that?"

"Spare us your artistic critique," said Montgomery. "For the benefit of Mr. Koko, who were they?"

Carlozo turned to look at me and told me.

"Yeah, thanks," I said. "I figured that out yesterday, after Fleming bought the farm. You should have leveled with me earlier."

Montgomery continued, "There was someone else traveling with Cannon & Crowley that year: yours truly. You wouldn't remember, Carlozo, because I wasn't a performer. Heavens, no. But I was there on the show, working the sideshow tent, fleecing the customers in a game of chance. I was what Mr. Koko might call a 'broad tosser'. A three-card monte man.

Perhaps not the loftiest of occupations, but we did well, and the management got paid their privilege, so I still thought of myself as an important part of the show."

"Cheating the locals was an important part of the show?" asked Carlozo incredulously. "That's the cheapest excuse I've ever heard."

"Don't play the choirboy; it doesn't suit you. That year, we met a few times, Carlozo, whether you remember or not. I ran a little poker game for the show folk. We'd play in the baggage car, during the long jumps between stands. You weren't much of a gambler, I'd heard, so I didn't give you much thought. But one night, you stopped in on the game, you and Bork and Fleming. After the stand in Pierre, South Dakota."

Montgomery shifted uncomfortably on his gimpy leg and continued. "I don't know if you'd been drinking that night, but it was true you weren't much of a gambler. In fact, you were *terrible*. Within an hour, you'd lost at least two months' wages with some of the clumsiest card playing I had ever seen. Frankly, I thought you were playing that way intentionally, to confuse everyone or get their guards down. And if that was your feint, you were overacting. But no, you were just *that bad*. Bork and Fleming were losing, but not as badly as you. And you and your ego decided the problem wasn't that you were an impatient buffoon who didn't bother to count cards, let alone figure the odds—no, you decided that I must've been *cheating* you. Are you remembering any of this now?"

The King of the Air stayed silent.

"You started grumbling about it, and getting Bork and Fleming madder and madder. It never crossed your mind how stupid it would be for me to cheat the kinkers in my game—they were my friends, my means of survival and transportation. To cheat them would be suicide. No, you, you self-important idiot, decide that I must be cheating, so you talk Bork and Fleming into redlighting me. You and your buddies gather me up, take the money I had honestly won—*honestly won!*—and drag me back to the end of the train. You

132

had your fun and jostled me around a bit, trying to scare me. Then you looked me in the eye, Carlozo, and laughed, and said, 'Hey, want to know what it feels like to fly?' And you and your buddies tossed me off the back of that train. Left me to die, in the middle of South Dakota, in the middle of the night. Just because you were a lousy card player."

While his voice spiked with emotion once or twice, mainly he narrated this event in a flat, rich voice. He'd rehearsed this in his head many times. He'd had way too much time to think about this, and plan.

"What of it?" Carlozo said finally, with his jaw sticking out. "It happened years ago. Ancient history."

"It's not ancient history," said Montgomery, "when every step I take shoots pain up my back like fireworks. It's not ancient history when I look in the mirror every morning and see the beard that hides my scars and my broken jawbone. It's not ancient history just because you *say* it is."

All eyes were on Carlozo, sizing him up as the kind of person who would do something like this. Redlighting was rough justice in the circus, and most of us had probably never seen it. I knew I'd never been this close to it before, and it gave me a shiver. Even Boots, judging from her stare, had never heard this story before. But the dye-job flyer stood tall and erect in his silky shirt, unrepentant on the surface, shameless to the end.

"I spent weeks in a podunk hospital, nearly dead, attended to by a quack who was drunk more often than not. But what else could I do? I had no money—you'd taken it all—and no one to call for help. So I stayed there and tried to heal. After that, I drifted a while, and eventually made my way to Top Town. It was a good place for me, I figured, with plenty of suckers to be clipped, flatties and kinkers alike. You see, I'd lost my scruples somewhere along the way. No one knew me back then, so with the money I earned, I made myself into a legitimate businessman. All the while, I listened for news of you and your daredevil buddies. I waited until you all washed up here, which you were certain to do.

"It was easy enough to ruin Bork and Fleming financially. But aside from taking their money, I also wanted to give them a feeling of desperation before they died. I had the Redd Brothers terrorize them a little, then sent them a reminder of South Dakota before their accidents. But the great Carlozo was harder. You still weren't a gambler, as far as I could tell, so I needed to get under your skin a different way. Luckily your massive ego and manly pride were still intact. And while you were hard to tempt into action, this roundheels wife of yours gave me the opening I needed."

"Watch it, shorty," I said. "You may be a con man, racketeer and murderer, but when you start insulting broads, you're gonna rouse the Galahad in me."

Montgomery looked at me with all the affection you'd spare a bedbug. "Carlozo, the presence of your little monkey here is seriously undermining the pleasure of my grand scheme."

"You've been reading too many pulps, mac," I said. "I'm waiting for you to twirl your mustache and give us an evil 'bwah-ha-ha-ha!' Come on, Carlozo, ain't you even going to stick up for your wife in this? Or is the sight of her gagged and tied to a chair an everyday thing?"

Carlozo wasn't looking at anyone but Boots. "It doesn't matter what you say about her. She's my wife. She may be a lot of other things, but she's still my wife. Give her back to me."

"My dear sir, I fully intend to," said Montgomery. "The only hitch is, you'll have to find her."

Both of us looked at Montgomery like we missed the punchline. Carlozo asked, "What are you playing at? Untie her now, or I'll tear to pieces." He hunched up his shoulders and took a step toward the old man.

"I'm sure you could," laughed Montgomery, "but you might find Missouri Redd here a more formidable opponent." The muscle from the Ozarks stepped forward as if in a beauty pageant for bums. "I have something a little more sporting

134

in mind, to make things more interesting. Now, just look at your wife there. So beautiful, so spirited. Quite a number. No wonder you think so much of her. She adorns your household, gives it its splendor. She's like a queen, in fact. So, we're going to play a game, a game of 'Find the Queen'. It shouldn't be difficult for a sharp operator like you. You just need to watch and listen carefully as we move her around, and then tell me where she is. Simple enough? All right, here we go!"

And with that, Missouri Redd turned and wheeled Boots back behind the striped canvases. The squeak of the little metal wheels went on and on, as if he were wheeling her all over the place, though the sound of the wind made it hard to follow. "Hold!" shouted Montgomery, and the wheeling stopped. He walked over to the curtain in the middle and parted it with his walking stick. There sat Boots, looking very confused. "And there she is. See, this isn't hard, anyone can win who can count to three." He dropped the curtain and shouted again, and the wheeling resumed.

"All you have to do to be a winner is find the queen. Only three spaces to watch. Keep your eye on where she goes and you win her back. Listen carefully for it. Hold!" Again the wheeling stopped. This time, Montgomery pulled open the curtain on the right side, revealing Boots again. Next to her, Missouri Redd was starting to look a little winded.

"You see, the game's almost too easy, there's hardly any sport in this at all . . ."

"Carlozo," I warned, "don't fall for this."

"The great Reynaldo Carlozo," he mocked, "taking the advice of a dimestore bigshoe. What do you say, Carlozo? Quit now, or get your wife back?" He dropped the curtain and the wheels began to turn again. "Listen for the wheels, Carlozo. You can find her. For all the trouble she's caused you, all the humiliation, you can find her. Shamed you in front of everyone, with her tramping around."

"*You* set her up for that!" I shouted. "You sent her to Bork's."

Everyone ignored me. "She's running around even now,

but can you stop her? Can you catch her? Find the queen, find the queen, and she's all yours."

The curtains were wafting slowly in the dim light. Carlozo was watching, looking for any tip that would give her away. Without saying a word, he had accepted Montgomery's challenge to beat him at this game. And like a thousand elmers before him, he was going to lose.

"Carlozo, wise up! No one ever wins at three-card monte! He must've gaffed this. You know he did!"

"Be quiet, Koko!" said the flyer without looking in my direction. "I need to concentrate."

"Whaddya mean? We can tackle these mooks."

"Forget him," the card sharp said, continuing his mesmerizing grind. "Watch the queen. Look for the queen, my friend. Easiest game in the world. Find the queen, you're a winner. Miss the queen, go home a loser."

I made a move toward Montgomery, but he pointed his walking stick at me and warned, "Take another step and she's finished, clown!" This guy was so bughouse, I had to believe him. I stopped in my tracks, with no clue of what to do. He'd set the hook in Carlozo and was going to reel him in.

"Find the queen, you're a winner. Miss the queen, go home a loser. You're a winner, Carlozo, always a winner. The King of the Air! Find your queen! Hold!" The sound of the wheels stopped. The wind moaned eerily through the factory. Montgomery said quietly, "Where's the queen, friend?"

Without hesitation, Carlozo pointed and said, "The left."

"Part the curtain, man, see if you're right."

Carlozo confidently stormed over, grabbed the canvas and took a step behind it. Then with just the slightest click, like the sound of a doorknob turning, there was a sudden whoosh of air. The canvas blew forward mournfully, and Carlozo was nowhere to be seen. Instead, his voice echoed vainly out of the open trap door, as he fell down a chute three stories to the loading dock. Then a simple thud, and nothing.

CHAPTER 21

Three Bullets and a Lady

The way I look at it, revenge is like a marzipan pickle. It looks like it'll taste a lot better than it really does, and waiting and thinking about it for 15 years doesn't help any. In his "victory", Montgomery showed all the emotion of a guy washing his socks, even as Carlozo was lying downstairs, dead or nearly so. The old man stood there, staring quietly at the curtain billowing over the hole that had sucked down Reynaldo Carlozo, the King of the Air. An egotistical, arrogant, cuckolded, short-tempered baby, sure, but also, by all accounts, the best flyer there ever was.

He moved his jaw and his dentures clacked again. "That was satisfying," he said, flatly and unconvincingly.

"Wouldn't a Coke have been less trouble?" I asked.

The natty schemer stood silently a few moments more. "It surprised me that Carlozo brought you into this, Koko," he said finally. "Why would he hire you to find his wife, when you couldn't find your way out of a bottle? I'd planned for him to go looking for her himself. I quite relished the idea of his public humiliation and witnessing the demise of the others."

"He had his reasons," I said. None of them very nice or noble, I thought to myself, but that was beside the point now.

"I guess we'll never know, will we?" he said with a grin. "Mis-souri!" From behind the middle curtain came the big roustabout, pushing Boots in the chair. She had her eyes closed tight, holding back tears. She'd seen the whole thing. When her gag was stripped from her mouth, she let out a throaty scream that people probably heard up in Skelton Heights. She wasn't frightened. She was fury personified.

"Oh my my," said Montgomery. "You're bound to strain yourself, my dear."

"You're crazy!" she yelled. "You're insane! Why would you kill a man for something that happened 15 years ago!?"

"Correction," he said, losing his mock-genteel tone. "I killed *three* men, and I did it because they tried to kill me, when I had done nothing wrong."

Boots could only respond with wheezing growls.

"Well, you sure put on a big spec for it," I said. "I half-expected prancing llamas and girls in feathered headdresses."

"I appreciate an elaborate production," he smiled. "The result of living among all you circus folk, I expect."

"A couple of quick shivs in the dark, and you'd've been rid of them. But now you've got a problem. The frustrated Ringling in you has made this a complete larry. You've left a trail bigger than 20 elephants, with a house full of witnesses. How are you going to keep yourself out of the noose?"

"By killing you and the woman," he said.

I considered that for a minute, then admitted, "Okay, maybe it wasn't a *complete* larry."

"Even a simpleton such as yourself should be able to understand," said Montgomery. "I'm practically untouchable. Money, used wisely, has that effect on people. Everyone who's played a part in this depends on me for something. If they turn me in, their lives will be ruined. So everyone keeps their mouths shut, because they have to get along.

And isn't that what makes someplace a community?" He smiled at his cynical wisdom.

"Lotta knows you had the Redds take Boots," I said.

"Miss Mudflaps wants to keep her precious club," he reminded me, "which will make her memory selective."

"What about Plummett?"

"Ha! He has less spine than anyone," he said. "Missouri, untie the woman. You see, Mr. Koko, this will all work out rather neatly, or neat enough for the police, whose distaste for Top Town I'm sure you're familiar with. You've been asking around town for Boots Carlozo. Now, you're very tight with your secrets, as was Carlozo. So what's to stop people from imagining that there was some sort of lover's triangle between you three—flyer, wife and clown? What a disgrace for the world's greatest flyer! He couldn't bear the shame and killed himself after doing the two of you in. And Bork and Fleming were obviously killed in a jealous rage earlier. That's the sort of story people like to hear and spread around." He looked at me like I'd be able to appreciate a plan that wrapped up so nicely, even if I weren't going to be around very long to admire it. People would buy into this story because it was what they wanted to hear. I thought of how, as much as I'd fought it, I fell for the gossip about Boots. Montgomery understood human nature more than I cared to admit.

Missouri Redd had untied Boots from the chair, but he kept the ropes on her hands and feet. Montgomery reminded him that this might look a little suspicious later when the police found the body. "If it's all the same to you," said Missouri in a cautious tone, "I'd like to leave 'em on and take 'em off when we're done."

"What's the matter, you southern fried chicken? Can't handle a little skirt like that?"

"Shut yer pie hole, clown, or else . . ."

"Or else what? You gonna kill me? Your boss already tipped me off to that little secret."

"Oh, I could make it worse, believe you me."

"What ya gonna do, breathe on me? Recite your multiplication tables? Tell me about your last fishing trip?"

Missouri's pig eyes narrowed down to the size of raisins. "That tears it, clown. I've taken enough from you." He let go of Boots, leaving her wobbling and reeling on her trussed feet. From inside his overalls, he pulled out his pistol.

"Missouri! I do *not* want him shot!"

"Especially not with that filthy thing," I added. "I worry about infections. Take it home and clean it so you can drill me properly."

"Jus' keep talkin'," said Missouri, as he aimed at me, "so I can shoot that red nose off your face." Boots pushed herself into his shoulder, trying to ruin his aim, but with her feet tied he easily brushed her aside. She landed roughly on her back, a foot away from the open shaft. His boss shouted at him again to stop. Missouri smiled with his yellow teeth, and slowly turned until the gun pointed toward Montgomery. The old man didn't flinch, even when a shot exploded and Missouri's gun went bouncing on the floor.

"Sorry about that," said a voice from behind us. "Hope I didn't hurt your hand."

"No, ya little show-off," said Missouri, shaking his fingers, "but ya didn't help my piece much."

Out of the shadows strode Texas Redd, with a confident smile on his face. He nodded to all of us like we were meeting at the church social, but he kept his shiny pistol pointed directly at Montgomery. "Ya oughta take better care of your pistols, Missouri," smiled his younger half-brother. "Else it'll get ya in trouble one-a these days."

Texas Redd walked over and helped Boots back to her feet. "Now brother, untie this poor gal. Hardly a gentlemanly thing to do, leave her like that." Missouri made a move to do so, but remembered the scratches on his face and stopped. Texas walked over and picked up the gun on the floor. When he saw how flinchy his half-brother was, he stuck both guns in his belt, called Missouri a fraidy-cat, and began to work on the ropes himself.

"What in God's name are you doing?" asked Montgomery. "Stop it."

"Sorry, Mr. Montgomery, I must follow the biddin' of m' heart."

"Missouri!" Montgomery shouted. "Stop him! Grab your gun, you fool! Shoot him!"

Missouri looked over with an offended look on his face. "Now, Mr. Montgomery," he chided, "I can't shoot him. He's kin."

"Okay, sheriff," I said, "you've got me officially confused. You're *not* trailing Boots?"

"Sure, I was," he explained. "Mr. Montgomery hired me to follow her and I suspected he was up to no good, but a job's a job these days. But once I started followin' Miss Adeline around, I realized what an angel she is, an angel sent straight from heaven. So naturally, him killin' her would upset me greatly. She wiggled away from me this afternoon, but luckily I was able to track her down agin."

Boots stared at him dumbfounded through this whole spiel. When the last of the ropes came off, the only thing she could think to say was, "Thanks."

He replied, "Ma'am."

"A' course," said Missouri, as if the idea took this long to congeal in his brainpan and burst into his consciousness, "since he's kin, I could just take him in a fistfight."

Quick as a flash Missouri Redd caught his half-brother on the chin with a right cross. It sent the cowboy reeling, and Missouri landed a couple others on his chin before he could defend himself. Instead of pained, Texas looked happy and eager to be invited to spar. In between punches, the two actually gave each other compliments on their shots and pointers about proper technique—"Get that elbow up earlier, boy, or ya got no leverage," "Hope ya got some raw steak at home for that eye." You'd think they were a couple of yahoos playing golf. Of course, such lessons rarely take hold when you're having your face redecorated, but one had to admire the pride in their craft.

I was admiring them so much, in fact, that I had forgotten about Montgomery. By the time Boots shouted, "Look out!" I felt his walking stick crack on my shoulder right where Maine had struck and fell to my knees from the blinding pain. Montgomery grabbed Boots and began to wrestle with her, trying to force her into the shaft that had claimed her husband. I got to my feet again, trying to focus my vision. Boots, stronger than the old man, was holding her own, but she let out a scream from the excitement. The Redd Brothers' fistfight stopped for a moment. Texas Redd pulled one of the guns from his belt, fell to one knee and fired off two shots. Montgomery let go of Boots and grabbed his stomach, falling backward onto his caboose. The pain of the impact brought a pathetic yelp out of him and he slowly laid himself down on the dusty floor.

Sweating and panting, Texas and Missouri Redd walked over and stood above the groaning figure of the con artist. From his trick shooting earlier, I'd guessed Texas made both of his shots count. The look on the old man's face was one of surprise and disgust. Missouri kneeled down and said, "Mr. Montgomery? Mr. Montgomery, you can't die."

Grimacing, Montgomery tried to speak but couldn't through the pain.

"You ain't paid me yet." He reached into the dying man's coat, took out his billfold, and helped himself to the cash inside. By the time he put it back, Montgomery was dead. So he helped himself to a pocket watch and some gold rings as well.

CHAPTER 22

Black Mariah

T.C. Montgomery was truly pitiful, lying there on his side, his nice green suit getting mucked up by warehouse grime and the dark, growing stain in his midsection. He might've had good reasons to hate Carlozo and Company, but nursing a grudge that long will give ya nothing but bloody nipples.

So, what was the next step? The four of us looked at one another like we'd made a date for badminton and forgot to bring the birdie. Montgomery's plan for getting rid of witnesses hadn't worked so well. Now the room had nothing *but* witnesses, and the man who was supposed to get away was lying on the floor in a lifeless pile. Without her scarf, Boots' disheveled blond hair hung down and curled like a protective hood around her face. She looked tired and confused, and I couldn't blame her.

Texas Redd, who showed no pain from the fight, looked at her and smiled a dazzling, white, milk-fed smile. He took a few steps in her direction, but she flinched and walked backward. So he stuck his pistol into his belt and cleared his throat.

"Miss Addie, ma'am," he started, with the sincerity of the greenest first of May, "everything I told Mr. Montgomery was true. I'm sorry I was tailin' you, but it was a job, an' my brothers were pushin' me to do it, 'cuz, y'know, it'd be a good thing for brothers to be in business together. Y'know, such things could lead t' somethin' better, like runnin' a truck farm or a service station. Turns out this business was deep down no good, and I had to double-cross m' brothers besides, while not crossin' you too much. Or not at all, I mean. But you wasn't . . . I mean, weren't to . . . but . . . ma'am . . . aw shucks. . ." He began to get tongue-tied.

For a moment, Boots couldn't speak. I was a bit slap happy myself by this point. All this plotting, revenge, brutality—and along comes a blushing, beguiling Texas Redd. In the midst of all this wreckage, all this poisoned energy, he pops up like a schoolboy with a crush on his teacher. It's like you're ready to toss the world onto a scrap heap, and you pass by a clump of bouncy wildflowers that brings a tear to your eye. I'd've been touched by this gink, if I didn't suspect he was touched in the head.

"Texas, please," said Missouri Redd, "I think I'm gonna be sick."

"Shut yer mouth before I come over and finish poundin' you," answered Texas, turning around.

"Finish?" mocked his half-brother. "When ya gonna *start,* boy?"

Texas made a move toward his punching partner, but Boots shouted, "Stop it! Stop it!"

"Ooops, sorry ma'am," said her suitor. "You're still upset, and I understand. If I'd'a known that Mr. Montgomery were plannin' to hurt your husband, I would've stepped in earlier."

"That's pretty stale bread now, Hopalong," I said. "Where was your compassion when you were beating the wax out of Carlozo and me this afternoon?"

"Stay outta this, clown! You got no stake in this."

"No stake? I've had to protect myself from falling corpses all day, and now all those angry poker players, plus you

144

Neanderthals. The cops need to hang this all on someone, and it ain't gonna be me."

"Neanderthal?" asked Texas.

"Sounds Jewish to me," said Missouri. "What you hintin' at, clown?"

We bickered back and forth, but if you want a match of wits, you gotta have wits to match. Amid the jabber, Boots walked over to the open shaft and kneeled down at the edge. When we noticed this, we shut our yaps and watched. A little respect was due. That was her husband at the bottom of the shaft, and despite everything that had happened, that still meant something to Boots. My guess was, she was trying to push aside the hidden history, the disappointments, the weak moments and the baby now inside her, and recapture the face of that daring young man who'd swept her up in the air so long ago. I've heard it's like nothing else, up there.

The wind continued to whistle through the factory, but the sound was now joined in a chorus by the high whine of police sirens. It was anybody's guess where they came from; maybe Lotta panicked and told them to find us here. The three of us on our feet grew agitated, while Boots calmly knelt by the hole. Then she frowned to choke back a sob, made a sign of the cross, and got back on her feet.

"I'm done with Top Town," she said in a strained voice. "I've let this place hold onto me for too long."

"No, wait," said Texas Redd.

"You pugs can worry about the police," she continued. "I haven't done anything wrong. I'm jumping a train out west, like I should've done before all this."

"What about your baby?" I asked. She pulled up short, surprised that I knew her secret. "How you gonna survive another afternoon like today?"

"Don't worry about me," she said, putting on her tough face again. "I'll feel better once I'm out of here and people stop chasing me. Besides, you think I want to raise my baby here? Where people will talk about her mother and all this . .

. this . . ." Whatever word described this, it escaped her. "Or she should grow up surrounded by worn-out circus bums and drunk towners, trying to figure out her place in this cheap spectacle? Fat chance. My baby's never going to see a circus, or ever hear about Top Town." She walked around the hole and headed for the door.

"Wait, Miss Addie!" said the love-struck wrangler. "You can't leave . . . I . . . I . . . I got an uncle with a ranch down by Fort Worth. I could take you there. It's a big ol' place, jus' beautiful. You'd love it."

Boots turned around and gave him an incredulous look. "What is the matter with you? Why the hell do you think I'd go anywhere with you?"

"Because I love you, Miss Addie! I do! You're prettier'n the sunrise over the prairie, and stronger than a Brahma bull. If you could forgive me for even bein' associated with that evil little man, I would try and make you the happiest woman alive. Please give me a chance."

"What about the baby? She's not yours."

Missouri snickered at this nicety. "Hardly matters in the Redd family. Kinda goes with the territory."

Boots paused to let this all sink in. For all her bravado, escape would be easier with a male companion and bodyguard. He was obviously tough enough, and couldn't show his true colors more if he stripped himself naked. But she'd so thoroughly convinced herself to go solo that the newer plan gave her pause. She turned to me with a pained look. "I can't go with him, can I? I've made so many wrong choices lately."

I smiled and said, "Hey, the law of averages might be with you this time. You wanted to get out into the open air again, with no crowds around, didn't you? A ranch sounds like a good place to do it. You're an old farm girl anyway. If you're leaving, you better go catch a boxcar now, because the paddy wagons will be here any minute."

She looked at the young roustabout, all red and rosy like a candy apple. He looked so excited, even his bruises looked good on him. Boots sighed and said, "All right, Texas, we're heading out." She turned to me and said, "You didn't make any of this better, but I know you were trying to help. So thank you."

I smiled a weary smile. "Send me a picture of the little bip when you can, care of the Club Bimbo."

Texas reached over and handed one of the pistols back to Mis-souri. Disappointed that their clem had been interrupted, they showed all the emotion of a pair of sleepy mules. Soon they'd realize their paths would cross again before long. It was Fate, like your bread falling jelly-side down. As Boots and Texas Redd headed through the door, escaping to a ranch didn't seem like such a bad idea at all. Maybe her life would simmer down, maybe it wouldn't, but at least she had someone along to do her heavy lifting.

Missouri Redd turned to me and said unpleasantly, "So, clown, it's down to me and you." He pointed the pearl-handled pistol in my direction.

"I know it's a romantic setting, Mizzou, but don't get any ideas."

He spat again, and this time hit my shoe square on target. "What's to stop me from pluggin' you right now and cuttin' outta here before the bulls come?"

I winked, then said, "C'mon, even you know the answer to that one."

He looked surprised that I'd give him any credit. "I do?"

"Sure you do."

"Can you give me a hint?"

"Aw, you don't need a hint," I joshed.

"Yeah," he said without confidence, "you're right."

"It's so obvious," I said, heavy on the butter. I walked over and put a confidential arm around his shoulder. "Think about it. I let your half-brother—who is one helluva guy, by the way, if I haven't told you—I let him escape back to Texas, with a fine pretty girl at his side. And you Redd Brothers stand up for kin, this much I know. That obviously means you owe me

147

one. Not to mention, nobody saw you gaff the equipment at Bork's or Fleming's, right? So that's water under the bridge. Follow me so far?"

Missouri blinked his eyes and grunted, "Uh huh."

"And here's the other thing," I told him. "You might not have noticed this. The gun in your hand? That's the one that shot Montgomery. Look at it. See? Texas gave you back the wrong gun, haha. What a boner! Now, if you shoot me with the gun that shot him, it will be obvious. The cops will pin it all on you."

"But what," he interrupted eagerly, "what if I shoot you and then get rid of the gun? Wouldn't that work?"

"Mizzou! Get rid of a beautiful gun like that? Look at it. Such workmanship, pearl handle. Just gorgeous. It'd be a shame to throw that away. And then anyway, you talked about cutting out before the police come. It's going to be really hard to run with those broken toes of yours."

He chuckled a little bit. "Ya big dope! I ain't got no broken toes."

Savoring this moment as long as I could, I looked him in the face, my arm still around his shoulder, for what seemed like an hour. I watched his face fill up with a dawning awareness like a balloon filling slowly with helium, then jumped with all my weight on his right foot. He screamed, and the lightly held pistol popped out of his hand. He tried to jump for it, but stumbled to his hands and knees. Knowing that even a hobbled Missouri might still tie me in a knot, I reached in my pocket and clumsily pulled out my own revolver. It felt awkward in my hand, until I turned it around and pointed the barrel at him. I picked up the pearl-handled gat and stuck it in my pocket, then motioned him to get on his feet and walk out.

The red-headed roustie limped down the stairs, muttering and cursing. We stepped through the office door to the out-side, just as a pair of paddy wagons pulled up. Their headlights blinded me for a second, long enough for

Missouri to reach around and yank my revolver out of my hand. The cops ran up, screaming for him to stop, as he pointed iron at me.

"Don't do it!" I shouted.

Missouri Redd smiled his mean little smile. "Never did like clowns," he said, as he pulled the trigger. With a measly click, out popped the red-and-yellow flag that read "BANG!"

"Huh. I didn't even know that thing was loaded," I explained, as the cops tackled us to the ground.

CHAPTER 23

A New Deal

In the bone-jarring ride in the back of the paddy wagon, I kept working on Missouri Redd to convince him that he'd have to come clean about Montgomery and Carlozo, or else I'd point the cops in the direction of that little ol' ranch in Fort Worth. In some perverse combination of family honor and thug pride, Missouri couldn't allow Texas Redd to be dragged back into this mess. Maine Redd was more tight-lipped than usual with me, so I couldn't tell if he'd go along or not. He seemed to be made of the same stuff as his brothers, though, and so with the cops he'd be as stingy with information as he was with pocket change.

They took the three of us all the way to the Dukenfield calaboose, along with a cabinet full of drunks and a bunch of mopes who'd slapped their wives once too often. We were the only kinkers at the station that night except for Swede Madigan, who was on such a bender that he kept calling everyone Mommy. This especially rankled his mother, who, having been pinched for streetwalking, was being booked along with the rest of us.

After a while the rousties and I were put in separate rooms. Mine was elegantly furnished with two bare bulbs in the ceiling, a table with two broken chairs, and white tile up the walls, sporting red stains which made me think, if you're gonna try and shave in here, at least bring a mirror. The atmosphere was enhanced by the aroma of many years' worth of cigarettes and sweat.

Over the course of the evening, various flatfoots popped in to pass the time and try to beat a confession out of me. Most of our conversations started with the words, "Go ahead, say something funny." Some were tougher than others, but usually it was no time at all until they were holding their sides, wiping their eyes and staggering back outside to catch their breath. Spaulding cops aren't as tough a crowd as they think they are.

Then in came the detective who spends his Christmas vacation getting in fights with department store elves.

"So, bigshoe," he piped, "we meet again."

"Evening, Napoleon. Whaddya hear from Josephine?"

"Take a seat. It's practically morning anyway. Quite a mess last night in the tent factory."

Piscopink was being annoyingly civil. Maybe he felt I was a lead-pipe cinch for the Iron-Bar Hotel, so he didn't have to overplay his hand. "Yeah," I said, "that's show biz."

"You wanna tell me what happened?"

"I got a choice?"

"Nope."

So I told him my side of the story, how I was hired by Carlozo to find his wife, how Montgomery was a murdering, vengeful galoot, how the Redd Brothers did his dirty work. I left out the three-card monte game, because the midget was already giving me the fish-eye. I also left out Texas Redd entirely, and whether I had ever found Carlozo's wife.

Piscopink lit a gasper and blew tantalizing smoke into the air. "Funny, that's not how the Redd Brothers say it happened."

"All that inbreeding must do something to their memories."

Piscopink snorted. "They say you had a personal beef with Montgomery, that you went to mess up his card game first, and when you didn't find him there, went to the factory to gun him down."

"I'd never been to that game before tonight. I had no idea he was running it until . . . someone told me."

"Why'd you go to the game at all?"

"The old ladies at St. Genesius kicked me out of their Bingo night. Got mad cuz I wouldn't tell them who dyed my hair."

Piscopink slammed his hands down, jumped onto the table, and before I knew it, had my collar grabbed in each fist. "Joke's over, Koko," he shouted, tipping me off-balance. "And so are you. We're not talkin' about a couple of circus stiffs now. Montgomery was a big fish around here, and not just in Top Town. He had friends in high places . . ."

"Then how'd you ever see 'em, with a periscope?"

He reared back to slug me, when someone grabbed his arm to stop him. It was his partner, Kashaw, who'd come into the room during the midget's eruption. Kashaw talked him off the table and into the hall. After a minute, they returned, Piscopink staring at me and breathing in hard puffs. Kashaw said, "Looks like you're free to go, Koko."

"Aww, I thought I'd get served breakfast."

"Maybe someday you'll get lucky," he said. "The Redd Brothers confessed to the killings, and their stories seem to jibe better than yours. You'll be called as a witness for their trial, probably, but until then we're done with you."

"I know you're in this up to your red nose, Koko," Piscopink said as I got out of my chair. "You're mixed up in this and I'm gonna figure out how."

Kashaw walked over and opened the door without saying a word.

"Don't leave Top Town," snarled Piscopink, "and watch your back."

I walked past and said, "For you, pal, I'll watch a little lower."

The cops at the front desk eyeballed me as I walked out. Their faces were strained and contorted as they stifled giggles. I couldn't have been *that* funny in the interrogation room, could I?

Then I noticed, on the bench and on the night sergeant's desk, copies of the *Spaulding Argus,* with a big, unflattering picture of me and Mayor Brody splashed across the front page. With my glazed expression and mouth hanging open as I passed out, I looked like I belonged in a jar of formaldehyde. As for Brody's forced smile, nervous eyes and cornered expression, you wouldn't trust him if you both fell off the ferry and he told you to start swimming. Despite their prejudices, the cops in the station couldn't reconcile the picture in the paper with me being a suspect in the murders. A stretch just too ridiculous for them to grasp. As an old boss clown once told me, there are many levels of ridiculous.

After some grumbling, the cops let me make a phone call before I left their lovely lock-up. Then, tired as I was, I walked the two miles from the far side of Dukenfield back to Top Town. The sun wasn't up yet, but its approach lit the streets dimly. The buildings around here appreciated it like an old bally broad appreciates a near-sighted boyfriend. The only gees on the street at that hour were the milkmen, the newspaper haulers and the hay balers headed for Bull Row and the Hippodrome. After all the commotion of the night before, I somehow expected Top Town to look different. But the faded banners still hung over the storefronts in the quiet air, promising thrills and chills to the empty sidewalk. The streets still smelled of whiskey, straw, horse piss and cotton candy, and the whole place was still eating itself alive.

I walked under the tattered canvas marquee that was the main entrance to Top Town. I continued down Grimaldi to our designated meeting place, but I was early for the appointment, so I loitered in a doorway nearby. After about 10 minutes, I saw Jimmy Plummett walking toward me. He didn't look too good, or too happy to be called out at this early hour. I waved at him from a distance, but he didn't respond.

"Top o' the morning, Jimmy," I shouted all friendly.

"What do you want?" he said, still a block away.

"I didn't want you to miss the sunrise, in case you wanted to write a poem or something." I went forward to meet him and pulled a broken axe handle out of a nearby trashcan. In my other hand was an old umbrella.

"The hell with that," he said. "What happened at the tent factory?"

"Oh, it was a bang-up time," I said, opening the umbrella as we stopped on the sidewalk. "You shoulda been there. The perfect end to this whole stinkin' larry. Montgomery and Carlozo are both dead, and Boots has skipped town. With any luck, she won't be coming back."

Plummett angrily smoothed down the hair at his temples. "How'd that happen? How come she got away?"

"Always the gentleman, eh, Jimmy? You should thank your lucky stars—and horseshoes and elephant hairs and little garden gnomes—that you didn't get pulled down into this, considering your part in it all."

"*My* part? What's bouncing around in that white skull of yours?"

"You were there when this all started," I sneered. "Jimmy Plummett, pimp to the stars . . ."

"You watch your . . ."

"You were the one who got Boots mixed up in this," I continued. "You passed her the mushy notes from Bork, which really weren't from Bork at all. Montgomery wanted them set up, and you were too happy to go along, especially after you slept with Boots."

Jimmy stared at me, fuming but not refuting, so I went on.

"You wanted to be like your idol, but you couldn't cut it. Whether or not you ever had your 'accident', you weren't a flyer. So, the closest you could come to being him was sleeping with his wife. And after that, you felt like such a louse you had no problem setting her up like Montgomery wanted. If she ran off, you could have Carlozo all to yourself. You might like to know, Jimmy, that Boots is pregnant, but I'm praying like all the teams at Notre Dame that it ain't your kid. I'd hate for a kid to start off life with something like that dragging him down."

Jimmy lunged at me, trying to get a hold of the axe handle, but I sidestepped him and raised it high. He flinched like I was going to bring it down on his head, but I brought it down on the bars of the building behind us. The apes in the Monkey Hostel were already awake, jumpy from our harsh talk, but banging on the bars really put their tails in a twist. Soon Jimmy was being hit with a deluge of food, both pre- and post-digested. He ran off in the direction he'd come, cursing me loudly, while I stood protected under the umbrella. I watched him run, lit a cigarette, and left.

I disagree that revenge is a dish best served cold. Fresh and piping hot, it has its own special tang.

I walked down Grimaldi a couple blocks and took a seat on the steps of the monument in Fratellini Circle, waiting for Top Town to wake up. Soon the kinkers would stir themselves, put the coffee on to boil, start the wash. I took the time to chew over a few things, not least of which was whether I wanted to walk these sidewalks again or crawl back into Daisy's stall and bury myself in the hay.

Then I thought about Texas Redd and that rare bird, Adeline Carlozo, and how far toward the open plains they'd made it since last evening. I guess a person's past can stretch back eight hours, 20 years and everything else in between, but a day only lasts from one morning to the next. I got up and hauled my carcass to the Pie Car for breakfast again. And this time, I could leave Rosie a decent tip.

155

PARLARI

advance – ahead of the show; here, used to refer to one's reputation

agent suit – clown's costume

all out and over – the entire performance has ended

Annie Oakley – a complimentary ticket or free pass. Famous sharpshooter Annie Oakley often gave free preview performances in town, shooting holes in playing cards. The lucky spectators who caught the cards would use them to get into the evening's show.

at liberty – unattached to any particular show

bally broad – women and girls who sang and danced in the circus spectacles

ballyhoo – the spiel shouted in front of the sideshow to attract attention

band organ – pipe organ designed for use in commercial public fairground settings to provide loud musical accompaniment to thrill rides and attractions

barbecue stool – electric chair

Big Bertha – nickname for Ringling Brothers and Barnum & Bailey Circus

Billboard wedding – a "marriage" for the duration of one traveling season that some circuses permitted between single men and women. These were considered as binding and exclusive for the season as a traditional wedding.

bip – child

blower – telephone receiver

boil-up – due to the lack of plumbing and hot running water, sanitation was often very poor on early American mud shows. Any day that the circus didn't play, all of the workingmen and the unmarried bosses would strip naked, "boil up" their clothing and take sponge baths.

Bombay horn – large brass horn with a rubber bulb

boner – mistake

broad tosser – three-card monte dealer

Bronx cheer – raspberry

bughouse – crazy

bull row – housing for elephants

bulls – elephants, whether male or female; police

bunce – profit

buried up to the axles – in your wagon, stuck deep in the mud

button – chin

buzzer – policeman's badge

carnies – carnival workers, to whom circus workers always felt superior

catcher – trapeze artist who catches flyers in the air

chippy – prostitute, promiscuous woman

clams – dollars

clem – fight, usually with townies

cloat – to steal

close ahead of paper – returning to winter quarters before the announced, or posted, end of the season

Clown Alley – area of a tent or lot where clowns put on their makeup and store their props

cooch show – strip show or burlesque show

cut up jackies/jackpots – to tell exaggerated stories, reminisce

donniker – toilet

drag clown – clown in female clothing

ducat – ticket

dukes – fists

dukey run – an unusually long distance

eel juice – liquor

elephant hair – talisman meant to bring good luck

elmer – townie, local resident

Feejee Mermaid – one of the most famous gaffs of all time, originating with P.T. Barnum, the supposed mermaid was the mummified head and torso of a juvenile monkey sewn onto the tail of a fish

finked – broken

first of May – rookie kinker, so called because that was when the season started for many shows

flatfoot – policeman

flattie – person; operator of a crooked game

flyer – trapeze artist who jumps across the air

funambulist – performer who walks on a wire

gaffed – rigged or faked

gasper – cigarette

gat – pistol

gee – man

geetus – money

gink – man

gin mill – tavern

glom – to grab, to steal

grift – confidence game, swindle

grind – spiel; a certain set of words used repeatedly by a sideshow talker or other hustler

grouchbag – purse that show people might wear around their necks. Interestingly, it may be the origin of Groucho Marx's nickname, as the early incarnations of his character in vaudeville were the ethnic stereotype of the "stingy Jew".

gunsel – gunman

guy wire – heavy rope or cable that helps to support poles or high wire rigging

guzintas – division tables; math skills in general

head south – to die

Hippodrome – arena for equestrian (horse) acts

hooch – liquor

hoosegow – jail

hostler – handler of baggage (work) horses

iron jaw – aerial act in which the performers work suspended by a mouthpiece clenched in their teeth

jane – woman

jill – woman

joey – clown, derived from Joseph Grimaldi, famous 19th century British clown

jump – distance between one performance and the next

kay fabe – secret information to be shielded from "marks" being swindled

kiester – traveling trunk

king pole – the first pole of the tent to be raised, which holds the peak of the tent

kinker – circus performer. Originally referred to acrobats, who needed much care and massaging to get the "kinks" out of their muscles

kip – sleeping place

larry – very unsuccessful date; broken toy or novelty; any fiasco or mistake

make your nut – to turn a profit. From the practice of local law enforcement confiscating the nuts off circus wagon wheels, to prevent the troupe from leaving without police authorization (and payoffs)

mark – target of a swindle

mitt camp – fortune-telling business or tent

mitt reader – fortune teller

moke – idiot

mook – fool

moolah – money

moxie – gumption, courage, determination

nanty – no, nothing

nautch joint – brothel

palooka – incompetent boxer; lout

patch – legal adjuster or fixer; to "fix" things with local authorities so that unlawful games and exhibitions can continue

plange – aerial act in which the performer's body swings heels over head while one hand and wrist are in padded rope loop

Podunk – small, unimportant, isolated town

ponger – acrobat

possum-back queen – prostitute, named for a type of storage unit built under circus wagons or railroad sleeping cars

redlighting – the practice of throwing a troublemaker or other undesirable person from a moving train (often between cars) in the middle of the night

Roman rings – gymnastic rings that hang from the ceiling or the top of a tent

roustabout, roustie – circus laborer

route card – the scheduled itinerary of a circus. The route was sometimes printed and sold to performers so their mail could be forwarded, but the danger of this was it might also tip off unhappy rousties and kinkers to places to disembark or find work with other outfits.

rube – yokel

runs – railroad yard

sawbuck – $20 bill

shiv – knife

simoleons – money

skejeema – money

skinner – muleskinner, someone who works with and drives mules

skirt – woman

slack wire – suspended wire for an acrobatic act that hangs loose and has some give and sway

slanger – trainer of big cats

spangleprat – derogatory workingmen slang for a performer

spec – spectacle, the opening parade of a circus performance

spiel – speech given by the talker in front of a show or attraction

spieler – announcer

spondulicks – money

spread – money

squeezin's – liquor, usually homemade

stand – any town where a circus plays

star-back seat – a reserved, more expensive seat

style – the "tada" pose, in lieu of a bow, that a performer assumes as a cue for applause

three-card monte – con game in which the mark is tricked into betting he can find the money card (for example, the queen of hearts) among three face-down playing cards.

three-sheet – three sheets of advertising paper, measuring 42 X 84 inches. Also, a self-serving performer with an overly high opinion of himself.

torpedo – mobster, killer

two bits – 25 cents

windjammer – circus musician

zany – clown

About the Author

James Finn Garner is best known as the author of *Politically Correct Bedtime Stories*, which was a #1 New York Times best-seller, and its two sequels, *Once Upon a More Enlightened Time* and *Politically Correct Holiday Stories*, both of which were also NYT best-sellers. The first book of this trilogy has been translated into more than 20 languages, and they have all been enjoyed around the world, including China, Japan, Poland, Indonesia and Iran. His other books include *Tea Party Fairy Tales, Apocalypse WOW!* and *Recut Madness: Favorite Movies Retold for Your Partisan Pleasure*.

His latest work is the *clown noir* mystery series starring "Rex Koko, Private Clown": *Honk Honk, My Darling; Double Indignity;* and *The Wet Nose of Danger*, as well as the holiday short subjects *A Very Rex Xmas* and *Have Yourself a Monkey Little Christmas*. These hard-boiled, big-shoed thrillers are available in print and electronic editions. In addition, *Honk Honk, My Darling* is available as a dramatic podcast, with all the characters performed by the author. Check out RexKoko.com for more information and a face full of fizz water.

Garner's writing has been published in *The New York Times, Playboy, TV Guide, Chicago Magazine,* and *The Wall Street Journal*, among others. His essays and stories have been broadcast on National Public Radio and the British Broadcasting Corporation. He is also a performer and a noted public speaker, especially after a few drinks. Some of these ephemera can be found at JamesFinnGarner.com.

He is the co-founder and custodian of Bardball.com, a website that aims to resurrect the art of baseball doggerel. Bardball is a fan-driven site that publishes new poetry every weekday during the regular season, and welcomes reader submissions, both lofty and lascivious.

CPSIA information can be obtained
at www.ICGtesting.com
Printed in the USA
LVHW021059250721
693626LV00011B/1057